THE DOOR
TO INFERNA

THE DOOR
TO INFERNA

an Elkloria novel

Rishab Borah

THREE ROOMS PRESS
New York, NY

The Door to Inferna
BY Rishab Borah

ISBN 978-1-941110-96-6 (trade paperback original)
ISBN 978-1-941110-97-3 (Epub)
Library of Congress Control Number: 2020935932

TRP-085

Publication Date: October 20, 2020

BISAC category code
YAF019010 YOUNG ADULT FICTION / Fantasy / Contemporary
YAF019030 YOUNG ADULT FICTION / Fantasy / Epic
YAF019050 YOUNG ADULT FICTION / Fantasy / Wizards & Witches
YAF019000 YOUNG ADULT FICTION / Fantasy / General

COVER ART: A. V. FLORES; www.avflores.com
KEY ILLUSTRATION: RISHAB BORAH
BOOK DESIGN: KG DESIGN INTERNATIONAL; www.katgeorges.com
DISTRIBUTED BY: PGW/INGRAM

Visit our website at www.threeroomspress.com or write us at info@threeroomspress.com

Three Rooms Press
New York, NY
www.threeroomspress.com
info@threeroomspress.com

Dedicated to my brother, who helped me a lot with this story,

and to my friend who helped me develop Neurazia,

and to my parents and my grandfather,

for encouraging me to finish this story.

THE DOOR
TO INFERNA

CHAPTER 1

Mysterious

IT WAS . . . SOME KIND OF party. Adults in odd clothes were dancing and singing. Embroidered, colorful robes, reminiscent of kimonos, swirled; swords hung at the belts of some—not weird at all—and adorning necks and wrists were bracelets and necklaces with intricate designs and gemstone inlays. Their faces were covered in unnatural shadows, preventing me from recognizing them. They threw handfuls of something sparkly in the air, while I watched and laughed. A voice in my head said, *They're not gonna want to hear about this afterward, are they?*

Whose voice was that?

I looked at the orbs hanging from the ceiling that lit the room with a dim golden glow, studying the dancing colors inside. I tossed my long blue braid over my shoulder.

Wait, long blue braid? I was dreaming again; the girl

1

was a recurring character. The girl who was always inventing strange devices.

I opened my eyes, pulling myself out of the dream. As I sat up, the sunlight threw distorted, golden rectangles across my rumpled shirt. I blinked at my surroundings blearily and my eyes fell on the clock. My mouth fell open as I realized I had exactly ten minutes to get ready for school. I threw off the covers and leapt out of bed. I scrambled toward the bathroom, tripping over my own feet—until I realized it was the first day of winter break.

I did my usual morning ritual and went downstairs for breakfast. My parents had made pancakes, sausages, and bacon. Their cuisine was fit for a king, honestly. I and every one of my friends knew it.

They weren't my biological parents—I was adopted. I never knew my real parents or even my real ethnicity. People told me I looked Latino because of something about the shape of my face and hair, though my skin was as pale as a vampire's. My real parents died long ago, and nobody knew how. I was only two years old when it happened. All I remembered was clumsily playing with and tangling up someone's dark red hair and an ominous roaring sound.

I wish I could meet my parents or at the very least find out why they died. I wish I could see whether they had eyes like me—*purple* eyes. Bright, shining, orchid-purple, just a little darker than magenta. Sometimes, it looked like they glowed in the dark. A thin, uneven, silver-blue ring surrounded my pupil, reflecting the color of whatever was around me. When I tilted my head a certain way and the light caught the silver ring just right, my irises seemed to flash gold. My parents apparently didn't have medical records, so my eye doctors didn't know whether my eyes were inherited or mutated.

I finished eating and turned on the TV. It was tuned to the news. My dad had probably been watching it, but I didn't change the channel right away.

The news was always the same—some country oppressing another country, someone else doing some corrupt thing. Every conflict seemed to happen because some huge, selfish country wanted the land of a smaller country, forcing them to fight to get more land.

I suddenly didn't feel like watching TV anymore. I told Mom I was going to the community center. She ordered me to put on some snow gear (it was snowing, after all), so I did and dashed outside. As I hurried down the street, I admired the snow-covered trees of the forest. The forest didn't have a name really—or if it did, no one knew it or bothered looking it up. It was just a bunch of trees we liked to ski between when it snowed. The forest usually looked dark and a little forbidding, but when snow blanketed the trees it looked like a winter wonderland enchanted with the magic of Christmas.

I stopped in front of Metara and Max's house. It had a frosty window and a dark brown door hidden in the little portico next to the garage. I ran up and rang the door-bell three times.

It opened, revealing a yawning Metara with a master-piece of a raven-colored bedhead. Her sleepy blue eyes focused on me.

"Hi, Metara!" I said rapidly—seeing the trees covered in snow always made me hyper. "How are you? Let's go to the pool at the Center! Wake up Max, okay?"

Metara groaned. "Slow down. It's too early, and I can't understand a word you're saying."

I carefully enunciated my words. "Pool. Center. Get. Max."

She snorted. "Okay," she said and walked back inside.

I smiled and waited for the return of one of my best friends. She's got a weird name, like me, but she always liked the name Metara and thought that any nicknames (like Tara or something) would be even weirder. She said Metara sounded like the name of a flower.

A door opened upstairs, and I could hear Metara's voice. "Max, wakey wakey! Come on, you need to take a shower! Khi's here. He's waiting!"

My full name is Khioneus Nevula. It's such a weird name, supposedly given by my biological parents, but it's a cool name, too. My adoptive parents' last name was Jackson, but I had chosen to keep the name Nevula, because . . . well, I didn't have a lot else left from my birth parents.

Upstairs, Max yelled, "Ow" in his high voice. Then he groaned, "Metara, you didn't need to hit me! I was already going."

Metara said, "Go faster. And don't forget your swim clothes!" Apparently my "Christmas magic" hyperness was contagious.

Metara appeared in the doorway, wringing the hand she had smacked Max with—did she seriously hurt her hand smacking him? "Max is getting ready," she muttered.

We waited for Max and after like five minutes Metara got impatient and went up to Max's room. I followed this time. Metara knocked on the door to the bathroom and whisper-yelled, "Max, get done already! Why are you taking so long?"

Max shouted back, "Jeez, let me shower in peace! Can't you give me a break for just one day?"

Metara said, "We're waiting!"

I whispered to Metara, "You can lay off him a little. Not everyone is all business like you. Some people use showers to relax."

Metara grinned and shook her head.

The water turned off, and Max yelled, "I'm done. Happy?" We waited downstairs as he dressed.

I felt bad about how much Metara harassed Max, but I had tried. Their antics were messy business—getting mixed up in them was never a good idea.

Metara dragged me outside, and we waited for Max again. He finally came down, his dark hair wet and a bundle of swim clothes under his arm.

Metara gave him a hug and covered him in kisses. "How is my wittle bro today?"

Max groaned. "Tar-tar, I'm older than you."

Metara rolled her eyes. "Only by seventeen seconds. We're *twins*! It's *irrelevant*. And don't call me Tar-tar, or I'll feed you to a bear."

"Where are you going to get a bear?"

"Technicalities. Let's get to the pool!"

"Both of you, quiet down," I said. "You'll wake up your parents!"

Metara frowned. "You're right. We don't want the Cranky Mom-ster and the Un-dad on the loose. Best to let them sleep."

Max sighed, giving me a look that said, *Could this girl get any more annoying?* I shrugged and smiled sympathetically.

Max, Metara, and I tell each other everything, and we know all (well, most) of each other's secrets, from phone passwords to worst fears. At school, people joke that Metara and I are girlfriend and boyfriend (to the jealousy of the many boys chasing Metara). Some even joke that Max and I are boyfriends. But really, we're more like siblings. We treat each other's houses like our own, and our parents don't mind us staying over at either house, even on school nights, as long as we do all our homework and get to school on time.

We walked to the community center and checked in to use the pool. We were the only ones there. I guess the idea of trudging through the snow to a cold pool didn't appeal to a lot of people, even if it was an indoor pool.

I jumped into the cold water, deliberately splashing Metara. Bubbles rushed up around me as I surfaced and shook out my sopping wet hair. Metara, wet from my cannonball, glared and jumped into the water close to me, splashing me in the face.

We laughed, then Max dove in and splashed us both. He surfaced with a goofy grin, so I smacked a wave of water at him. As I swam away from Max, I suddenly saw a spider floating near me.

Screaming, I kicked away from it. I clipped Metara and crashed into the side of the pool. Max just sighed and got a net to scoop it out, but before he got to it, the water rippled out around me, creating a huge wave that caused the spider to go flying into the air. I looked around frantically for it. Fearing it was somewhere on my body, I pulled at my swim shirt and checked my swim trunks, until I was mostly satisfied it wasn't there.

"That was weird," I said. "Was that, like, a jumping spider?"

Max and Metara were staring at each other, silently communicating something.

"What's that shady look for?" I said, swimming over to where Max was squatting on the side of the pool with the net.

Max frowned. "What look?"

I scowled at him, but he just shrugged. "Are you pranking me?" I asked.

Max's eyes widened. "What? No!"

I frowned. He sounded genuinely shocked that I would assume that. But what was that look for then?

Eventually, we returned to our game, but I made a mental note to confront them about it later.

⚜ ⚜ ⚜

THAT NIGHT, WE WENT TO A party at my cousin Hannah's house. There were video games, snacks, a movie, a dance floor, and several games like Truth or Dare. (Ugh, I hate dares! They're always stupid or dangerous or embarrassing, and when you don't do them, everyone laughs at you and bugs you about it.) I didn't dance—knowing me, I'd trip over my feet or something—but after much pressure from Metara, the three of us sang karaoke in a corner.

After the party was over, we walked home with a flashlight. Our parents trust us to walk without an adult, so it was all good, but I don't like the dark very much. It wasn't even late—only around eight—but it was still dark and cold. I admit, I was a little scared. Okay, more like *really scared.* I completely freaked out when I saw a cat's eyes shining in the dark and Metara had to shine the flashlight on it to scare it away.

After leaving Metara and Max at their house, something seemed more ominous about the night, and it wasn't doing anything good for my nerves. The moon was a quarter full. Or three-quarters empty, I guess, like something had eaten most of it—a cosmic monster.

Tonight, three-quarters empty seemed more appropriate than three-quarters full.

Something about it just made me nervous. It wasn't my fear of the dark—it was the kind of nervousness you get before something unpleasant and painful, like a shot.

My head began to hurt. Redness washed over the white of the moon, and a strange face materialized in the empty black space. It seemed vaguely feminine, though it had fangs and glowing purple eyes. It smiled at me and I suddenly felt like I was about to be the next meal of whatever ate the moon. The blood drained from my face. I couldn't tell whether I was imagining it, seeing some scary astronomical phenomenon, or hallucinating because of some bad food. An eerie voice floated through my head.

Come to me, unrealized one.

Suddenly, a flash of white appeared on the moon, and the dark voice disappeared.

More white flashes. Asteroids? Was the world ending?

A woman appeared in front of me. She wore a glowing white dress, and her long, silvery hair floated around her head. Beautiful butterfly wings sprouted from her back, with intertwining designs along them in many colors. Her blue-green eyes showed age and experience, though she didn't have a single wrinkle.

She bowed to me, and then took off into the sky, her wings flapping. I watched her go, but she disappeared when I blinked. The night seemed brighter then. A glow surrounded me, driving away the darkness. A shield of safety.

Sparkly fairy ladies. So . . . definitely a hallucination.

I ran home, shut the door to my room, and put my back against it. Then I slid down to the ground, breathing shakily.

⚜ ⚜ ⚜

AM I GOING CRAZY? I THOUGHT as I stood under the stream of water in the shower. It had been an hour or so since those hallucinations, and I decided I felt unclean and stressed.

So, a shower it was. Maybe a bath would have been better.

I looked up at the ceiling and thought, *Why am I hallucinating? I should talk to my parents about this, but . . . what if they think I'm crazy? Where are these hallucinations coming from? It can't be school. School work isn't that hard. Ugh, I hate having to wake up and go to school . . . Why am I thinking about that? I was trying to think about something else, wasn't I? What was it? Oh yeah . . .*

My train of thought went like that for a while, a dazed snake trying to find its way through a field of corn that all looked the same. I tapped my foot, and suddenly slipped and fell into the shower's bathtub. I jumped up, rubbing my rear, when something caught my eye on the bottom of the tub.

It was the face that had appeared on the moon!

The porcelain was morphing into the moon vampire. I yelped and stomped on it, pain shooting through the bottom of my foot.

I dashed out of the shower freaking out, sopping wet, and looking at every corner and shadow nervously. The face was gone—I told myself I probably just imagined it.

Nervously, I finished my after-shower and bedtime rituals and then dashed straight into my bed, pulling the warm covers comfortingly over my body, shivering but not because I was cold.

I still couldn't stop myself from looking around the room nervously, into the corners where the walls and ceiling met and at the closet door. My eyes fell on the mirror at the foot of my bed. The surface was rippling like water! And if that wasn't freaky enough, it reflected a sliver of light from a gap in my window curtains. Too much light. The moon wasn't that bright tonight, and my window faced the forest, not the street.

I sat up in bed, reaching over to grab the curtains. Pulling them back, I peered out of the window. Multicolored lights danced between the trees.

I fell back on my bed, freaked out again. The mirror had stopped rippling.

Why? Just . . . why? All the unusual things I had experienced—hallucinations, odd dreams—were they all connected? Did this kind of thing happen to everyone?

I pulled the blankets up to my chin. Suddenly, a memory of the fairy woman's ageless face and blue-green

11

eyes flashed into my head. I immediately felt safe, as if she was watching over me.

Obviously, she was a hallucination—an unpleasant thought that killed my feeling of safety. I would talk with my parents tomorrow. Maybe they knew of a non-mental-condition reason that I was seeing things—like stress or food poisoning or something. That idea calmed me a little, and I finally drifted off to sleep.

I had another strange dream that night. I usually only had a few vision-dreams a year, so two in a row was odd even for me.

I was sitting on a windowsill far above the ground, so high that the deep green hedge maze beneath me looked like a drawing. Luckily, I don't have a fear of heights . . . I think. It's a . . . "sometimes" kind of thing. Like, sometimes I can walk on a platform above four thousand feet of empty space and think it's cool, like when I was on the glass bridge at the Grand Canyon. Other times, I'd be on a high balcony scared stiff. Maybe it's because you can actually see the ground from the balcony and imagine the injury you might get, whereas the view on the glass bridge is almost, well . . . unreal—like if you fell off, you'd just float down.

A gibbous moon that was way smaller and bluer than it should have been hung in a purple night sky among glittering clouds. It was like someone had decided there wasn't enough color in the sky, so they added a bunch. I idly wondered whether the world of my dream had a different moon phase cycle, because in the real world the moon was a quarter. I had never seen the sky of my dream-world before.

The thought fluttered away. My dream-self sighed contently and gazed at the tiny blue moon. I looked at the sprawling gardens below me. Hedges formed maze-like patterns around circular beds of purple flowers. Large, silvery trees waved in the wind, leaves glittering slightly in the light of the gibbous moon. My eyelids drooped as I drifted off.

Right as I fell asleep in the dream world, I woke up in the real world. I looked out the window. It was still dark. The clock said it was five in the morning. Why had I woken up so early? I was such a deep sleeper that I needed an alarm to wake up before *eleven.*

I got out of bed; as awake as I was, I wouldn't be able to sleep again. I grabbed a book and snuggled back under my covers to read.

A few hours later, I had finished two books and wanted breakfast. I dressed, brushed, and went down to meet my parents for breakfast—cream of wheat.

At noon, after doing some much-needed chores, a truck rumbled outside, and I ran to the guest room window.

There was a large moving van in front of the house next door. That house had been empty for weeks, ever since the previous family moved away for a new job.

I put on a coat, hat, and gloves and went out to see. Someone was already on the porch—a girl with platinum blonde hair and green eyes.

She smiled at me. "Hello. My name's Sarina."

"Hi. I'm Khi. It's nice to meet you."

She was looking directly into my eyes. I was waiting for the moment Sarina noticed their strange color and did a double take. She never did.

Sarina pulled out a plate of cookies from behind her back. "Here, these are for you and your family. Particularly for you." She winked.

Flustered, blushing and unsure how to take that last comment, since I had pretty much zero experience with flirting—especially not with people that forward—I accepted the cookies. Another girl walked up behind her then. This girl also had platinum blonde hair but was taller than Sarina and had blue eyes. There was a definite resemblance between them.

She must have noticed the redness of my cheeks, because she sighed and said, "Sara, do you always have to torture the neighborhood boys? You really could lay off for once."

The second girl looked over at me. She didn't do a double take at my eyes either.

Still blushing, I said, "Uh, do you guys want me to show you around the neighborhood or anything? Introduce you to people? Sorry, I didn't get your name yet."

"Oh, I'm Sammy," the second girl said. "It's nice to meet you. You don't need to show us around—not to be rude, but Sara and I prefer to meet others on our own. And, sorry about Sara's flirting. My twin sister isn't very subtle. Some people are flattered by comments like that but not everybody."

I smiled uncomfortably and nodded. I suddenly didn't want to live next door to Sarina at all. I felt bad for even thinking that, but it was how I felt. Sarina and Sammy were twins, just like Metara and Max. Two pairs of twins in the same neighborhood. What a funny coincidence.

That evening, I decided to see if Metara and Max were free to hang out. As I walked toward their house, something seemed to draw me into the forest, and I found myself walking toward it.

Voices whispered between the trees. I stopped, not wanting to disturb the voices. A strange curiosity came over me. I have never really been nosy, but some part of me wanted to know who was whispering and what they were talking about.

The voices seemed to whisper faster as I moved deeper into the forest. The snow crunched squeakily under my feet. Suddenly, a shaft of light hit me in the face. A red glow shone between the trees, and my heart leaped into my mouth. Was the forest on fire? I was scared, but I had to investigate the light. I walked into the trees. The whispers seemed to come from all sides now. I looked around frantically but could see no one. Soon, I found myself in a clearing, but the glow was . . . gone. The whispering stopped. The clearing was empty except for a large rock in the center.

I sighed. "It disappears just like that. Abracadabra. What is going *on* with my head? First, I see demons in the moon and sparkly fairies. Now this? Next thing, I'll be seeing unicorns."

As I talked to myself, something else happened—something completely inexplicable. Light spilled from the rock, as if every dust particle on the surface of the stone had become luminescent.

Then, as if by magic, the stone moved. It split in two, part of the stone floating up with stone columns materializing underneath it, making a sort of archway. In between the columns hovered an oval of darkness.

My brain couldn't process what I was seeing. Where had the columns come from? Was it some kind of hologram? Did that technology even exist?

Was this the entrance to a government base, hidden by advanced tech unknown to the public eye? A wormhole? Or was my mind just spinning out crazy theories and all this was just a film set?

I walked around the thing. The oval was actually an ovoid—an oblong sphere. I reached out to touch it and felt nothing, only cold, like sticking my hand into mist. So it wasn't a hologram? What would happen if I reached the center of the thing—this hole in the fabric of reality or whatever it was?

I wasn't ready to risk putting my hand into it, so I picked up a pebble and threw it into the darkness. It flew into the center of the ovoid and then disappeared.

I ran around to the other side to find it, but it was gone.

Okay. Wow. It wasn't a hologram thing or some sort of

film set. The wormhole theory was more likely. But how was it here? Government technology? Extraterrestrials?

I knew it was dangerous, but I just had to know what happened if my physical body entered it—my curiosity was so great that it overruled my logical mind. I reached my hand into the dark sphere. When it reached the center, my hand disappeared.

I screamed and yanked my hand back. It was still intact. Nothing had happened to it. Encouraged, I tried again, putting my hand in further. I felt a strong sensation in the hand that was gone. It was cold but not cold, as if it was so hot that it felt cold—but without the pain. It felt like my hand was vibrating, as if on a jet in a hot tub. It actually felt kind of good.

I concluded that stepping into this black hole . . . wormhole . . . whatever . . . wouldn't hurt me—unless it was a portal into the radiation-permeated, atmosphere-less, unforgiving void of outer space or something.

Maybe I should take some time to think about this. I could try throwing a walkie-talkie through and see if I could communicate with it—but did walkie-talkies work that way? Or what if I got a drone and flew it through to see if it could fly it out again? I'd have to borrow a drone from my friend, Alex. Would Alex would mind if his drone got lost on the other side of a wormhole?

I turned to leave, feeling hesitant. Maybe I could bring someone to check the wormhole out with me.

But what if the wormhole closed while I was gone?

In that pause, something that wasn't my own brain compelled my legs to turn my body back around and walk toward the portal. I tried to stop, but I couldn't. It was like something had possessed me. Hallucination was nothing compared to being unable to control my movement.

My traitorous legs stepped into the ovoid, and my disobedient hands went into the vanishing point, pulling my body through it, my hands pushing on a surface that I could not feel. As I passed through, images flashed in the darkness around me: the Taj Mahal, a hellish fiery-orange sky, a strange city with sleek buildings and flying cars, and many more images—some earthly and some definitely not. My arms finally pulled my whole body through, and I emerged on the other side. I felt very hot, and my legs began tingling. My hands suddenly let go of the surface I could not feel, and I fell head-first but not in the direction dictated by gravity. Where was the gravity? Wait . . . there was no gravity! I wasn't falling, I was *rocketing* forward! Was that heat I felt some sort of propulsive energy blast? Where was I going?

Air rushed past me, and suddenly I was in what looked like some kind of interdimensional funhouse. All around me, I saw reflections of myself. It was like a three-dimensional mosaic made of . . . me. Was I spinning? I felt dizzy.

Suddenly, a spot of light shone in front of me. I rocketed toward it and was ejected out the other side into another place.

CHAPTER 2

A New Place

I TUMBLED ONTO HARD DIRT. I lay flat on my back for a second, trying to get used to the new direction gravity was coming from. Then I realized I had control over my body again—with that realization came a wave of nauseating motion sickness.

I rolled onto my side and retched, though nothing came out. I gasped and pushed myself up, using my arm to brace myself.

I was still in the forest, but the snow had vanished—melted or evaporated, I didn't know. The air seemed sweeter, but thinner and not that cold. Everything seemed more colorful.

Then I noticed that all the trees were wrong. Some looked like metal sculptures. Others had odd, multicolored leaves, and still others had fruits I'd never seen before. I was not in the forest back in Truckee. How had I gotten here? More importantly, where in the world was I? Or . . . where *out* of the world? Had the wormhole or whatever taken me to a different planet? A different dimension?

Something rumbled to my right like a stampede. The ground shook slightly, the trees swaying. Suddenly, several people on horseback burst out of the trees. I dashed out of the way and hid. As I got a closer look, I realized they weren't riding the horses—they *were* the horses. From the waist up, they looked like men, women, and children in toga-like clothing, but from the waist down, they were horses and foals.

They were . . . centaurs. I could barely process what they were saying, as I crouched behind the tree.

"Quick! Everyone keep moving!"

"The Ker is coming! Move on, move on! Seal the Norikithintes Portal!"

The herd rushed on while two centaurs stayed behind and began chanting, their hands glowing. The archway, the sphere-thing of darkness, still hung in the sky. A luminous circle appeared in the doorway, containing a bunch of strange symbols that looked vaguely Chinese. Rings of symbols and geometric shapes surrounded the circle, with more appearing each second. Some of the symbols used English letters, but others looked Greek or Hindi. They formed themselves into rings, hexagons, triangles, squares, and stars. A shimmering like heat distortion hung around the archway. More circles appeared around the door, four of them opposite to each other on different sides. The dark sphere shrunk and dissolved into nothing.

No! What are they doing? I thought. *That's my only way home!*

The centaurs galloped away, and I ran to the archway. The luminous circles still hung in the air, rotating slowly. I reached my hand toward the archway and hit something solid, the force of the impact sending needles of pain up my fingers. The symbols in the center of the circle distorted into a shape like an eye that peered at me narrowly. I stepped away from it, creeped out.

This was some really advanced technology, and that eye thing in the center of the symbol circle was super weird. Was it a camera, watching me? I had heard of technology that used sound waves to move objects or create invisible containers, but those only worked on things like marbles. This . . . was different.

Could it be magic? I pushed that thought away. Magic was silly. All of this could be explained by some sort of science, I was sure of it.

I sat down and sighed. What would my parents think when I didn't come home?

They might think I was kidnapped! I had to get back home.

I looked up at the sky. Strange bands of color stretched across the sky. They were *rings*—like *planetary* rings.

I wasn't on Earth anymore. I had somehow traveled across space (or maybe time) to another planet entirely using the wormhole. Maybe I should just call the wormhole a "magic" portal.

The sun had been setting back on Earth, but now it was still high in the sky—a little after noon. The sun seemed almost double the size it should be, and the light it shed was too orange.

I heard a whispery hissing sound. I jumped up and saw a strange smoke seeping between the trees. But it was too black to be smoke—dark and oily.

"Who are you?" said a voice from the darkness. It sounded like a hissing snake, a vacuum cleaner, and a crackling fire all at once.

I backed toward the archway, my shoulder blades hitting the smooth, invisible wall. The darkness slithered forward. I wondered if this was the "Ker" that the centaurs had been yelling about. It certainly put me into the same kind of panic.

"The pattern of your ionic waves is tainted. Born in one world but lived in another . . . " A tendril of darkness formed into a snake's head with glowing purple eyes. It came closer. I moved aside, still pressing against the invisible wall, until I stumbled backward where the wall ended abruptly. I dashed behind the archway.

"WHO ARE YOU?" The voice increased in volume.

"Get away from me!" I cried as the snake slithered through the air toward me.

It opened its mouth. I stumbled back as black fire poured from its mouth. More snake heads popped out of the main body. They hissed and several lunged at me. One of them swallowed me whole, dropping me in darkness.

Suddenly, a blue light tore away the darkness and the snake head recoiled with a roar that sounded unnatural coming from its thin body.

Someone grabbed my arm. A voice whispered a strange word—"**Rappidum**." I turned but I couldn't see the speaker. I heard more strange words and turned again. Suddenly, everything blurred as I shot off through the trees—literally through the trunks of the trees. I felt like the Flash and would have thought it was pretty cool if I hadn't been scared out of my wits.

Someone ran alongside me, but I couldn't make out their face, until we stopped in a clearing, and the person turned toward me.

My jaw dropped. "Max!?"

He gave me an interesting look, a mixture of relief and weariness. Metara appeared next to me, and I jumped like a foot in the air. "Metara!?"

I squeezed my eyes shut and reopened them. Metara and Max still stood there, amused smiles on their faces. I vaguely noticed that their hair wasn't the right color— Max's hair was blue with silver ombre and Metara's was purple—but pushed that oddity to the back of my mind so I could focus on more important things like . . .

"What the heck was that *thing*?" My anger at their amusement overwhelmed my shock for the moment. "It tried to *kill* me! Why are you guys laughing?"

Metara's grin faded. "I guess we need to explain. You aren't in Truckee anymore, nor are you on Earth. You're on Pyrhithya, another planet in another universe."

I sighed. I had suspected that, but it was different entirely to hear it said out loud. I sat on the ground. In a matter of minutes, my entire perception of reality had been turned upside down. How and why Metara knew all this was another mystery.

"You traveled through the Norikithintes Portal, back in that clearing. You were born here, on this planet. You were sent to Earth as the first in an experimental program, to protect wizards like you from that dark being, whom we call Triskén."

"But those Centaurs called it the Care or something," I said.

Metara nodded. "Yes, it has many names, such as the Ker, which is what the Kentauroi call it."

I frowned. "Slow down. So I've traveled through some portal thing, to a different dimension."

"Universe," said Max.

"Universe, then, and to another planet called Pylhith . . . Pynhym . . . Pyskith . . . whatever it's called, which is actually where I was born. So I'm an . . . alien then? And I lived on Earth because wizards like me—wait, *wizards*? Okay, the world and everyone in it has gone crazy. Or maybe the world was always crazy, which is normal to everyone because they're crazy, so I am the only crazy one because I'm normal . . . so . . . so . . . agh!"

Metara giggled. "Maybe going through the portal made your head wonky. Khi, you're a *wizard*. You have *magic* powers, bestowed upon you by the celestial gods."

What did she mean by that? Nobody was *serious* when they used the word "magic." She had said *gods*, too. What was she talking about? I thought she was an atheist.

Actually, at that point I couldn't have cared less. I had seen Centaurs and snakes made of smoke. Metara telling me that magic existed confirmed what I had seen.

More importantly, how long had Metara and Max known about this alternate universe—how long had they kept it from me? *Why* had they kept it from me?

I took a deep breath to calm myself down. "Magic, huh? All right, whatever. I can use magic. Didn't some famous person say something about how advanced technology can be indistinguishable from magic? I'll just believe you for now and pretend you guys are explaining something about super advanced technology. So . . . why am I here, anyway?"

Max gave me a pensive frown. "You said the trigger word *abrakadabra*, with a "k," allowing someone born in Elkloria to open the Norikithintes Portal."

Metara grinned. "Why did you even say abrakadabra? Were you secretly practicing in the forest to become a stage magician?"

I burst into laughter. I felt strange, almost manic. I had never laughed like that before, and I didn't like it. "Abrakadabra. I literally just said the word abracadabra while talking to myself . . . Okay, I'm going crazy. I'm dreaming. I'm hallucinating. Maybe I'm dead. What the heck is Elkloria?"

Metara said, "Well, there's a simple trick to see if you're dreaming." I yelped as she pinched my arm.

She sighed. "Now do you think it's a dream?"

"Fine, then," I said. "Show me magic. I'm sorry I'm being mean right now, but I'm so confused. I don't have any spare brain power to be nice."

Metara said, "No feelings hurt. I know you're trying to wrap your head around something extremely hard to believe."

Then she held out her hand and whispered, "**Illusy Ashbirrus.**" A cheeseburger appeared in her hand. I held out my own and it floated over to me, plopping itself down in the center of my palm.

It looked so delicious and inviting. I could almost taste the beef, but . . . it wasn't actually there. I couldn't feel its texture on my hand. It was just floating there, like a trick of the light or a hallucination. Maybe a hologram. Technology indistinguishable from magic, right?

A second later, it disappeared. I looked up at Metara, confused.

She said, "That was an illusion spell. It's something sorcerers can do—sorcerers of Elkloria. Elkloria is the great land, the united country."

"You sound pompous when you say that," I said.

She rolled her eyes. "What caused you to say abraka-dabra right next to the portal anyway? You've never even been to that part of the forest."

I frowned. "There were these . . . whispering voices and this flickering glow between the trees. I thought it was a forest fire, so I went to investigate. And when I was near the portal, I said abrakadabra because I was, uh, talking to myself. I said something like, 'Abrakadabra, the glows and voices are gone.' Then my feet moved on their own, forcing me into the portal. It was like I was possessed or something! Anyway, now I'm here."

Metara's eyes widened. "A possessor wraith!"

"A what?"

"Do your thoughts feel sluggish?" she said. "Do you have pain in your head? Do you feel like something is trying to get inside your mind?"

I frowned. "No, no, and . . . I don't think so?"

Metara put her hand on my forehead and muttered something. "Your mind feels fine."

"What do you mean?" I said. "Did you do something?"

Max gave me a grave look. "Someone must have sent a possessor wraith to force you here. The wraith is gone, but the fact that someone sent it means you're not safe. We've gotta take you to Neurazia immediately."

He grabbed my arm and held his hand out in front of him like he was a priest conferring a blessing or a wizard casting a spell—which was exactly what he was doing, I realized.

"Wait!" I said. "Slow down! Who's Neurazia?"

Max turned. "You mean *what* is Neurazia. It's one of the elemental kingdoms of Elkloria, the magical kingdom of the mind. You are the prince of Neurazia."

"I'm a WHAT?"

"The question there is *who* are you, not *what* are you." Max winked. "You're the prince. You were sent to Earth when you were two years old. Our family was sent to protect you. But your sister stayed here, because she is the elder and next in line for the throne. I think that you're supposed to be protected on Earth in case your sister is killed by Triskén and a new ruler is needed, but I'm not sure what the exact reason for the Triskén Defense Program is."

"I'm a prince? I have a sister? Next in line for the . . . throne? Your family is supposed to protect me? How can you be from Elkloria?"

"We need to get to Neurazia. We'll explain stuff there." Max seemed restless, but I didn't want to go without a clearer explanation.

"But . . . Earth! My parents! My life! Are my parents in on this whole magical kingdom in another universe thing too? Are they protectors as well?"

"Don't worry, Khi. They know all about Elkloria and will cover for your absence. They protect you, just like we do. They don't have magic so that it is harder to find you, so Metara, our parents, and I do most of the protecting."

"But I want to go back home!" My voice cracked. *Everyone* knew about this, and no one had ever told me? It was like a conspiracy. Did everyone else in Truckee know about it too?

Max sighed. "We'll go back Khi, I promise. It's just . . . the Kentauroi have sealed the trans-dimensional space between the universes now. We'll have to wait until it's unsealed tomorrow. We also need to create new shields around your house after the unsealing. The seraphic protection put upon your house has dissipated, as it was fueled by your ignorance."

My body sagged with relief. I'd be going home tomorrow. I didn't know what the seraphic thing was that Max was talking about, but I hoped it would be sorted out.

"But right now," Max said, "with the possessor wraith obviously sent by Triskén, it would be best to get to Neurazia, where you'll be safe. And your real parents will want to know that you're here."

"My . . . what?" I whispered.

"Your birth parents are alive. They're the king and queen of Neurazia!"

"You just made my life *so* complicated."

Max smiled. "Well, it's time to uncomplicate it a bit, Khi." Then he said, "**Transporta**." His voice echoed strangely, not like the acoustics of a forest.

Then everything around us melted away into purple mist.

CHAPTER 3

My Parents

THE MIST CLEARED. WE STOOD BEFORE an enormous, free-standing archway in the middle of some kind of patio. Odd symbols were etched into the frame. All around us were beautiful gardens, full of a variety of flowers, hummingbirds, and surprisingly big butterflies.

Wait a second. Those weren't butterflies. They had butterfly wings but . . . they looked like miniature humans. Fairies? They were like little people in tiny clothes with wings and elfin features and colorful, prismatic eyes.

Max caught me staring at the little creatures and said, "You can admire the pixies later. Right now we have somewhere to be."

He turned to the archway and said, "*Imaginaria seit-eyeh exia res keyava.*"

A kind of thick, white mist filled the archway. Strangely, it never strayed from the portal but hung inside it.

I frowned. "Was that a password?"

Max shrugged. "Neurazia is a bit of an isolated kingdom. Outsiders can only enter if they have a permit or if they know the key and have Neurazian genes, like us."

I walked through the mist. I felt an odd, tingly sensation like I had in the portal in the forest. Suddenly, the three of us stood in a small hallway.

I followed Max and Metara into a large, circular room. There were five doors along the curved wall, and in the center of the room was a sort of glowing pad. As we walked forward, a man appeared on the pad. Teleportation? Holographic projection? Astral projection?

Was magic just advanced science? Were magic and technology based on the same scientific laws, whereas magic simply utilized scientific concepts that people from Earth hadn't discovered yet? Or were the laws of nature simply facades for . . . something else?

The man walked over to me, bowed, and spoke with a British accent. "Good day, I am Marco. How may I be of service to you all?"

Max walked up to the gentleman and said, "We would like to go to Layer Palacia."

The man nodded. "You are all citizens, so you do not need to fill out any forms. Right this way."

There was a diagram on the wall. It showed five gray bars of different sizes, one above another, with the middle one being the longest and the top and bottom the shortest. Each bar was labeled in three languages— English, something that looked like Latin, and some strange glyphs I couldn't understand. The English labels said things like "Layer Palacia" and "Layer Reyuli."

I turned to Marco. "Um, excuse me, sir, what is that?"

He smiled. "Neurazia is a unique province, placed in a pocket dimension or 'alterspace.'" He pointed at the top-most bar on the map. "Imagine that this universe is like a large cloth, and Neurazia is located in a fold of that cloth, closed off from the rest. Without magic, anything going by the fold would simply pass over us. Neurazia itself is composed of five layers sitting on top of each other, all floating in a synthesized void. This top one is where we are. It's called Layer Vintilo, the entrance layer for those visiting Neurazia. Many of our hotels and restaurants are here."

He pointed to each layer in turn, describing their cities, people, trades, and cultures, until finally he reached the last one. "Lastly, we have Layer Palacia. This is where the Palace Imagicetra is, where the royal family and monarchs of Neurazia live. Like the rest of Elkloria, Neurazia has a system of royal lineage. That is where you are headed, is it not?"

Max confirmed with a dip of his head. Marco bowed. "I am glad I could be of service."

Marco guided us to the rightmost doorway in the room. My first thought was that each door must lead to a

THE DOOR TO INFERNA

different layer. No, that didn't make sense. That would mean the first door led to Layer Vintilo. But we were already on Layer Vintilo. What was the door for then?

"That door leads to the rest of the layer," Max said.

"Let me guess, mind-reading magic?" I said casually, with a grin. Then a thought struck me: how many times had Metara or Max read my mind back on Earth? It was an unnerving thought.

Max raised his hands placatingly. "I'm not reading your mind. That's a level of skill I don't have." I sighed with relief.

The door in front of us opened like an elevator, revealing a small, circular, green room.

The man nodded to us. "Please step inside."

Not knowing what to expect, I stepped into the tube first. Max and Metara followed. As I waited for whatever was going to happen, I turned to Metara and asked something I'd been wondering since we arrived.

"Metara?" I said, my brow furrowing slightly. "Why is your hair . . . purple?"

She smirked. "That's what happens when people travel between universes. When a Vhestibulian comes to Usifia, their hair takes on its Usifian color, and when a Usifian goes to Vhestibulium, their hair changes to its Vhestibulian color."

"Vhesti-what? Usi-what?"

Metara grinned apologetically. "Usifia is Elkloria's universe. Vhestibulium is Earth's. Sorry. Look here."

She muttered something, and a mirror appeared in her hand. In it, I saw myself for the first time since I arrived in this world. My wavy hair wasn't the brown with streaks of blonde I was used to. It was vibrant crimson with streaks of 24-karat gold. My head looked like it was wreathed in flames.

"Whoa!" Even the sparse hair on my arms had turned red. "This is so weird!"

Marco cleared his throat. It was only then that I realized the doors were still open and he was patiently waiting for us to finish our conversation. Max said, "We're ready to go."

Marco smiled. "Enjoy your stay in the province."

The doors shut. I turned to ask Max a question when the ground disappeared underneath us. I screamed, shooting downward through a transparent green tube. Metara and Max whooped behind me. A flash of light temporarily blinded me. Then everything went dark. A sliver of light appeared at my feet. The light grew until I was blinded once again, but this time I saw a blur of green, right as everything went dark and light again.

After my vision returned, I saw a blur of red and yellow. I got an impression of what might have been a house before I was plunging into darkness once again.

This time we stopped. I felt dizzy and a little motion sick. My feet rested on a solid surface, and a chink of light appeared, growing wider as the doors opened. I stumbled out of the tube. Max and Metara were right behind me. I took several deep breaths and finally panted out, "You guys really could have warned me."

Max looked ahead at something I couldn't see. "Let's go to the palace."

"Wait," I said. "You guys said that my parents are alive and that . . . I have a sister. Is that really true?"

Metara raised her eyebrows. "We wouldn't lie about something that big, Khi."

I frowned. "The thing is, you've been lying to me my whole life, haven't you? I just don't know whether I can trust you guys anymore. You hid this entire world from me my whole life—your whole life. I don't know how you could have lied to me since we were little kids, but my world just turned upside down, and you expect me to blindly believe you?"

I saw the hurt looks on their faces and felt bad. It was hard to be mad at them, but I had to know the truth.

Max spoke quietly. "We couldn't tell you if we wanted to. We had, well, enchantments on us that stopped us from saying stuff. But we've always been—and always will be—your friends."

I sighed. I believed them. They were my best friends. If they kept Elkloria from me, enchantment or not, they had a good reason.

"I forgive you guys. I'm not sure I understand, exactly, but . . . well . . . you've stood by me most of my life. You've always been there for me."

I was a little surprised at my willingness to forgive them, but it seemed right. But then . . . of course I would forgive them eventually. Even though there was a whole side of them—a whole world—that I didn't know about, they were still my friends. I had trusted them my entire life. Treating them as traitors, well . . . that would just make me angry, suspicious, broken. It would destroy me. Besides, if they were bad people, I would have noticed, wouldn't I? Having known them my entire life?

Metara sniffled a little and turned away. "Thank you, Khi."

Max said, "We're sorry. Neither of us would ever betray you. I swear."

I sighed and finally turned around.

I saw the palace.

It was magnificent.

It had about ten towers with conical roofs. There were even some floating towers connected by sparkling bridges. The whole thing was symmetrical. The walls of the towers had swirling floral designs and stained-glass windows including two large, green, glowing, flower-shaped buildings on either side of the main palace. The walls glittered in many different colors, not gray stone like a medieval castle. The palace was surrounded by a long, low wall. The air above it shimmered strangely.

Looking at the wide, silvery, cobbled path to the main gate, I forgot for a moment about going home. I wanted to explore this magnificent palace. Max grabbed my hand and pulled me forward. "Yes, it's awesome, but come on! You need to meet everyone."

He pulled me up to the large gray door. The door's surface began to glitter strangely, coalescing into words: *Welcome back, Maximillis and Metara Arigmorina, protectors of the Vhestibulian prince. Welcome, Princcens Khioneus Nevula. You are back at last.*

"What's 'princcens'?" I asked.

"'Princcens' is the title that people use to directly address a prince in Neurazia," said Max.

The doors opened, and Max and Metara took me through. We followed the same cobbled path, but now there were hedges around it.

Metara and Max took me to another set of doors. These were wooden with fancy gold trim, though for some reason, they still shimmered like metal, an inconsistent glow made from moving particles in the wood. On either side of the door were stained-glass windows with pretty designs made from diamonds and squares. The designs slowly changed color as I watched.

Max placed his hand on the door. The particles rippled at his touch, and a loud doorbell melody blasted out. Eight chimes rang, the door opened, and a slight girl with brown eyes and straw-blonde hair peered out.

"Hello," she said. "Who are you three?" She had the same accent as that Marco guy.

Another girl appeared behind her—tall, thin, and extremely pretty. She had braided, shiny hair the same cerulean blue as the ocean but with gold streaks like mine. She had a soft, curved face and a dainty body but brilliant gold eyes that told you not to mess with her. She was the kind of girl that shallow guys back home would chase after only to get brutally rejected. Luckily, I wasn't shallow, or I'd have found myself in an awkward situation.

The blonde girl put one hand out and another near her collarbone, both with palms facing up. She bowed and tilted her hand toward the blue-haired girl. Then she walked back inside.

"Metara?" said the blue-haired girl in surprise. "Max?"

She and Metara locked eyes, and for a few seconds, they shared a silent communication. The blue-haired girl turned to me, her expression joyful, her eyes wet.

"You . . . wait . . . " she breathed. "Isn't it supposed to be next year . . . ? Khioneus, is it really you?"

I responded with a tentative, "Yes?"

Suddenly, I realized the strange memories and dreams I had in which I was a blue- haired girl . . . that was her. Could she be my sister?

She hugged me, and murmured, "You're back, brother, you've finally come. I've waited twelve years. Finally. You . . . " She pulled away. Then she cleared her throat and, speaking more formally, said, "Hello, Princcens Khioneus, I am Princcentassa Khyonessa Nevula, Princess of Neurazia. You are my twin brother. Welcome to the Palace, and welcome home."

My mind spun with strange thoughts and emotions, mostly confusion, but love had also woken underneath, a love I never realized was in me. She hugged me fiercely again, my legs almost buckling in surprise. I hugged her back instinctively. "My sister. You're my sister. Where have you been all my life?"

She whispered, "I could ask the same of you. But I know where you've been. Still, I always missed you."

My sister. I had a sister. Khyonessa. I couldn't believe it. Suddenly, I didn't want to go home.

⚜ ⚜ ⚜

KHYONESSA AND I WENT INSIDE. METARA and Max followed. When we stepped into the entrance hall, the first thing I noticed was the tapestries on the walls. They depicted strange scenes—battles with armored knights fighting dragons and chimeras. Beautiful chandeliers dangled above. Under my feet was a purple carpet with intricate floral designs in gold. Large banners hung from the high, arched ceiling. Every banner had the same symbol: a golden eye with two lines curving from the top and bottom, right above and below the cat-like pupil, and three horizontal lines curving from the sides.

The wallpaper was also floral, but it moved, the flowers seeming to bloom and bud, gold becoming purple and purple becoming gold. Some—though not all—of the tapestries moved as well. They looked as if a camera were panning across the fights depicted. I wondered if the walls and tapestries were TV screens. No, it's magic, stupid.

Khyonessa groaned as we walked. "The throne room is so far! Mind if I use my teleporter?"

I shrugged, not knowing what to expect. Metara snorted and muttered, "Typical Nessa."

Khyonessa pulled out a small, silver ovoid with an antenna, a screen, and a keypad. She pressed a few keys and hit a big gray button. Then she grabbed Metara's hand, who in turn reached for mine as Max did the same.

"So, we're graduating from fantasy to sci-fi, now?" I muttered.

"If you think about it, they tend to be the same thing," said Max. "You realize you're basically an extra-dimensional alien with the same biological makeup as a human who can transpose vibrational signals between transcatenated particles to manipulate metatergetic energy in order to change the sequence of natural phenomena to your liking."

I stared at him. "I think I lost you at 'transpose.' I didn't even know that was a word." I hadn't understood much of what Max said, but I suddenly remembered how I had thought that magic was advanced technology when I came here. Had I been right this entire time? The device hummed. Khyonessa said, "Jump on three!"

"Why?" I asked.

"The teleporter won't work if you don't. It uses tactile links to teleport everything touching it but has a

THE DOOR TO INFERNA

maximum threshold for processing power. One . . . two . . . three!"

We all jumped at the same time. For a second we were suspended in the air, and suddenly, we were somewhere else.

It was a large, circular room with floor-to-ceiling stained-glass windows on one side (color-changing again) and two fancy thrones of purple and gold on the other. The ribbed, vaulted ceiling showed beautiful mosaics of forests and rivers that seemed to flow. On the floor was a massive mosaic of a man with red hair and purple eyes— like me—and a mustache and beard. The man held a staff, and a bird perched on one of his fingers. Deer and rabbits surrounded him. The trees in the background waved in the wind, and the sunlight seemed to glow. The man himself was motionless.

Metara looked at me. "What do you want to ask, Khi?"

"How do you always know when I have a question?"

Metara snorted. "I know you really well. You know I do."

I sighed. "I was just wondering who that man is in the mosaic."

She nodded. "That's Acutorias Nevula, your ancestor, the greatest Neurazian mage of all time, and the fourth greatest mage who ever existed."

"Fourth greatest?" I asked.

"He was behind Merlin, Yesus Christus and Sens Yoryos. I guess we could include Vivian and Morgana on that list, but they were evil, so I don't think they count.

Acutorias Nevula created the kingdom of Neurazia. People believed he was a Semideus—a holy magical being with powers beyond those of a normal wizard, like prophesying, infinite magic power, the ability to neutralize magic, and the power to turn into a god. But the idea of such a being with such powerful abilities is usually considered a myth."

A smirk came to my lips. "You know what you're saying right now makes no sense. I don't even know what you mean by 'god.' Everything I've seen so far should be mythical, so why shouldn't this Semideus be real too?"

"All will be explained in time," said Metara with a shrug. "Of course, not for a while." I raised my eyebrows. Why not now? Things still weren't completely making sense.

Right then, the air above the two thrones seemed to distort and shimmer, and a man and woman appeared. The woman had straight, dark blue hair that reached her knees. The man had light, wavy, red hair with gold streaks, just like mine—and now I remembered that his was the hair from the only memories I had of my parents. They were both attractive people and wore these fancy kimono-like shirts and flowy pants. They wore elegant crowns that bore several glittering gemstones of many colors.

They looked at me. Tears filled the woman's eyes. "Khioneus. Oh, Khioneus. You have come home at last."

"Are you . . . my parents?"

The king—my father—smiled. "Welcome home, son."

Emotion overwhelmed me. I was so happy that tears came to my eyes, and I could hardly breathe, warmth radiating through my entire body. My parents. My fantasy of meeting them had come true. They were alive. Real. They hugged me, all three of us together.

My joy was cut by a flash of sadness and anger. They had left me and kept my sister. At least before I had found out about Elkloria, I could imagine they didn't have a choice in the matter, they had to leave me because they had died. Now I knew they had chosen to give me up.

I pushed those feelings away, letting the happiness of reunion envelop me again. Dwelling on resentment wouldn't get me anywhere, and there was a reason I had been sent away—the Triskén Defense Program, though I suspected there was more to the story.

"You guys are my real parents." I whispered. "You're alive."

My mother whispered back, "Yes, Khi. We have always been here, watching over you. We never left you."

Somehow, the fact she knew my nickname made me feel ridiculously happy.

My legs wobbled as fatigue overtook me. The events of the day were catching up to me. My father seemed to feel my unsteadiness and whispered something to my mother— not a Mom and Dad like I had at home, but a Mother and Father.

He said, "Nessa, why don't you show Khioneus his room? It seems that fatigue from being propelled along the fourth- and fifth-dimensional axes has set into his system." He turned to me. "You could get sick if you don't rest."

Khyonessa—Nessa—turned toward me. "Come on. Let's see your room."

I was surprised. "But I'll only be here one day, and then I'm going home!"

Nessa frowned. "But you'll come back, won't you? You have so much to learn, history and magic . . . "

"I'm gonna learn magic?" How had I forgotten? I had magic powers!

"Well, obviously!"

I felt conflicted. On the one hand, I wanted to go home to my adoptive parents and my friends. On the other hand, I really wanted to spend time with my new birth parents and twin sister and to learn magic and explore this amazing world. "Will I have to go back to Vhestibulium?"

"Definitely," said my mother.

I frowned. "What if I don't want to?"

My father sighed. "You can't just up and disappear completely! If you did, the Vhestibulians would wonder what happened. And you still have school, with normal non-magical education! The math and science education here is far ahead of the math and science on your planet. Not to mention, you need to learn about the histories of both Vhestibulium and Elkloria. I assume you'll come to Elkloria when your school is on break."

I sighed with relief. A compromise. I'd get to come here, spend time with my birth parents and sister and learn magic, but I'd also get to go back to my world and my home.

I suddenly thought of my friends on Earth. Would I be able to keep the secret of this other universe from my friends? If I didn't, I'd probably go to a mental asylum. Even if they believed me, they could end up going crazy from the revelation and going to mental asylums themselves.

Nessa took me down a bunch of high-ceilinged hall-ways and up staircases. I stumbled sleepily after her. Every wall was covered with pictures and tapestries, and I noticed that the tapestries were almost 3D, with shining sunlight, swaying trees, and slowly moving clouds.

The palace was enormous. How was I going to navigate it?

Nessa took me down a long hallway that sloped up and down like a hill, stopping at a large silver door with no handle or knob. "Enrique," Nessa said, "come meet your roommate!"

CHAPTER 4

Spellcaster

THE SURFACE OF THE DOOR SHIFTED. A guy's face appeared, made from the silvery metal of the door. He had a mischievous smirk and a playful arch to his eyebrows. He looked like he was about twenty years old.

"What's up?" he said. "I'm Enrique. It's a pleasure to meet you, Princcens Khi."

"L-likewise, um, Enrique."

Inside, I thought, *The door just talked to me. Why did this stuff still surprise me?*

The door opened. "Come on in," said Enrique.

Nessa said, "Well, I'll be leaving now. Bye, Khi."

"Bye, Nessa." She smiled when I said "Nessa." Then she left.

I walked into the room. The door—Enrique—closed behind me. His face was on both sides of the door. He said, "I'm going out with my GF, Juanita. You should get acquainted with your room. I'll be back in a short while to talk."

Enrique's face disappeared. GF? Doors had girlfriends?

I explored my room, my earlier fatigue suddenly gone. The room was fairly big, with gray walls, a carpeted floor, and a blue bed with another stained-glass window above it. This window bore the design of a sun shining above a forest clearing. A large wardrobe stood next to the bed. On the other side of the room was another door—without a face, probably because it was the door to the bathroom. The bathroom had blue-tiled walls and a mosaic of floral designs on the floor, which, of course, changed color. The shower was huge and there was a bathtub as well. There were even different kinds of soaps and multiple shower heads.

I looked in the wardrobe. There were several fancy outfits in there and little doors in the back labeled "underwear" and "nightclothes". Well, at least I knew where to put my clothes.

I closed the closet and looked around. The room felt empty.

I decided to try and sleep, not wanting to get sick from the fatigue I felt in the throne room. I looked in the underwear drawer and found several pairs of silk boxers with gold trim and sequins. I put on some dark blue ones. They were more comfortable than they looked—the sequins didn't itch like I had expected them to. I tossed my Earth clothes on the floor. The room was so empty, it just felt right to put something on the floor.

I lay on the bed and stared at the ceiling, thinking about the ceiling murals in the other rooms of the palace. If I had one, what would it show? Maybe a picture of Max, Metara, and me hugging.

"I know that critical gaze. I've seen it on many people. You wanna redesign your room, don't you?"

I sat up in surprise, looking around until my eyes alighted on the door. Enrique was watching me. I turned red as I realized I wasn't exactly decent. I pulled the bed covers over myself. "What happened to your date? And can you knock . . . or something, next time?" Enrique laughed. "You were admiring your amazing but plain room for longer than you thought—my date's over."

Once again momentarily surprised by the concept of a door date, and mildly embarrassed, I could only nod. Enrique said, "Wanna know how you can personalize your room?"

I tilted my head, feeling curious. "Okay, how?"

"You have two options. You can use my power, as the door to your room, or you can do it yourself."

Both options sounded intriguing. "What do you mean do it myself?"

"Well, you're a sorcerer, so you've got magical transformation spells handy. You can fold your room into an alterspace, so you can change its dimensions, personalize it, or create things in it—whatever you want! You can make your room completely your domain. It's a very powerful spell."

I raised an eyebrow, studying his face. "What on Earth— Pyrgi . . . Pyrfi . . . Pyrhip . . . Agh! What in the universe makes you think I can cast such a complex-sounding spell? I barely even understand the concept of magic!"

Enrique smiled. "Learning basic spells is . . . well, it's supposedly easy. You concentrate on the desired outcome and say the words for the spell. I don't know exactly. I'm not a sorcerer, but all the actual sorcerers make it look easy. Come on, try it. Maxim Spacio Intero."

I closed my eyes and imagined what my room would look like. Way bigger, with blue walls, window drapes, carpets, maybe even with a few armchairs floating on clouds—but with other small clouds to catch you if you fell—and a floating bed with, like, stairs leading to the floor. I always wondered what it would be like to have a floating bed. Oh, and, the door should have a partition in front of it so Enrique wouldn't see me changing or anything. And the lights could be, like, chandeliers with floral designs. And a bedside dresser for books and such, and of course, a bookshelf. Maybe a desk. Oh! And a mirror, just like at home.

"Maxim Spacy . . . Spacio Intr . . . I'm not pronouncing this right. What's the spell again?"

Enrique enunciated each syllable. "MAX-im SPAC-io IN-tero."

I tried again. **"Maxim Spacio Intero."** My voice echoed strangely, as if I were talking into a microphone with reverb.

I felt something strange in my arm, as if tiny creatures were running from my shoulder to my hand. Startled, I opened my eyes.

The feeling disappeared, and I frowned. I had lost the image of my new room in my head. I tried again. **"Maxim Spacio Intero."** Once again, my voice echoed.

The feeling of tiny creatures on my arm came back, and my hand glowed. Something hissed, and my palm felt clammy. It became difficult to focus on the image in my head. A boom blasted from my palm and the wetness was gone. Streams of light flowed from my hand. Each stream went to a different place: one below my body and the blanket to the bed, another under the bed, still another to a place on the wall . . . each stream of light went to a place that I had wanted to change in my head. And then, everything changed. The walls pushed outward, carpets hissed into being, cushy armchairs—exactly how I imagined them—appeared near the bed, a dresser and mirror materialized, the bed rose into the air, an empty bookshelf grew out of the ground, and a short wall divided the room from the door.

"Hey!" said Enrique. "What's this for?"

"Sorry!" I said. "I just wanted a little more privacy!"

Then it hit me. I had literally cast magic—changed the shape of the room with my mind and words, bringing my imagination into the physical world. I looked down at my hands in wonder. Back in Vhestibulium, I'd be a Merlin, a Jesus, a Moses! I could change reality with my hands—not even my hands, just my voice! Could I split the Red Sea too?

Could I turn water into wine?

"I have the powers of a god!" I winced even as I said it. Max had once said to me that pride was dangerous in great quantities because the higher you regarded your-self, the lower you regarded others.

Behind the wall, Enrique said, "You really don't. Don't let magic get to your head. It may seem powerful, but it can be finicky. It also follows a rigid set of rules. Real gods don't follow rules—they make them."

Suddenly, fatigue washed over me and I fell back on the bed, too tired to think. I vaguely registered Enrique saying, "Rest up, Khi. You conjured a lot today." Then my eyes closed, and I drifted off.

❖ ❖ ❖

"KHI. KHI? KHI!" EARLY MORNING SUNLIGHT filtered in through the windows, washing my eyelids with red. I opened them to see Nessa hovering above me. She smirked. "The sleepyhead's finally awake? About time."

I groaned. "Don't yell at me. And you're not supposed to come in here unless I let you! That's an invasion of privacy."

She rolled her eyes. "It's morning. You're going home today."

I yawned and sat up. Nessa had quickly become the annoying older sister I never had. She whacked me lightly on the head and said, "Come on. Get into your robes for breakfast. Royals and nobles have to wear robes. Nice MES by the way."

"Mess?"

Nessa gestured around her. "Your magically enlarged space. It's really good. Did Enrique give you a spare amulet? I never found one with a cloud theme."

I frowned at her. "I made it."

She was taken aback and looked around again. "Huh. Who showed you?"

"Enrique," I said.

"Since when is he a wizard?" she said, looking at the door.

Enrique's face appeared. "I was made by a wizard. And you wizards—especially you, Nessa—use a lot of magic. Non-wizards pick a few things up."

Nessa floated down to the floor and out of the room (which was when I realized she was floating to reach my new bed). I made a mental note to tell Enrique not to let her in anymore, then I got dressed. The clothes were all strange. There were robes that looked like kimonos—like the ones my parents had worn and pants that all flared out at the bottom. I found some red pants and a white robe with gold trim. It took me a while to figure out how to put the robe on. There were buttons under the lapel inside of the robe, so I had to wear it with the left lapel over the right. The robe also had a belt. There didn't seem to be any regular shirts to wear underneath. Morning ritual done, I went to the door.

"Hey, Enrique, do you know where the dining hall is?"

Enrique appeared. "I can open a portal to the dining hall if you want. I can open a portal to any named door in Palace Imagicetra—except for the secured ones like in the congressional room."

I grinned. "That's pretty cool. I'd like that, please."

The door opened, and instead of leading to the hallway outside, it led straight into the dining hall. The dining hall was long and had large stained-glass windows depicting plates of food slowly being eaten (like, bites disappeared from the food, and when the food was gone, more would fall on the plates). Rings of orb-like lights floated near the ceiling. The long table was covered in a white tablecloth with gold trim, like my robe. Of course, the gold trim changed color—purple, blue, red, and so on.

There weren't many people around the table—only Nessa, Metara, and Max.

Metara patted the seat next to her, so I sat down. She pointed at the empty space in front of me and muttered a long string of words. I recognized the words spirit, breakfast, and December, but the rest was nonsense to me. Her voice echoed like mine had when I had changed my room.

I had cast a spell. It was still super-duper cool to think about. I could be a superhero!

I could be cooler than Superman!

My attention was immediately diverted by a puff of cyan smoke in front of me.

A plate of food appeared, complete with bacon, sausages, pancakes, and funny, multicolored apple slices. There was a glass of orange juice too. I looked at Metara in surprise, again. Where had these come from? Could I learn this spell?

"I bought these at a restaurant a couple of hours ago for you. The palace kitchen doesn't really specialize in American foods. Try the Spiritine apples. They're really good."

So, it was some sort of magical shipping thing. What currency did they use in Elkloria, anyway? Dollars? Rupees? Pounds?

As if she'd heard my question, Metara said, "We don't have Earth currencies. We use Taisumis and Inkoriallis. Since everything's magical here, we don't use physical currencies and instead have systems similar to computerized bank accounts. Most stores sell amulets for non-magicals that conjure up what they buy, and conjuration-spell contracts called Ablettis hor Conjuroa for wizards, so no one needs to carry things. It's convenient in that you don't have to stock up on things, I suppose."

I looked down at the food, resigned to the idea that my friends would always figure out what I was thinking with or without magic. I grabbed my fork and dug in, wondering if non-magicals ever found wizard powers unfair and wanted to revolt. Or maybe they were too scared? I hadn't met many non-magicals.

I bit into a slice of the Spiritine apples. Flavor exploded in my mouth—sweet, with a taste like . . . springtime. I didn't know what spring tasted like until now, but that was the only way to describe it. My head filled with images of blue skies, flowers, and chirping birds.

Nessa said, "They taste delicious, don't they? Too bad they're so hard to get. They're harvestable under the spring moon . . . which is why they taste like . . . well, springtime. Anyway, the portal has reopened, so you, Max, and Metara will be going soon!"

My mouth was full, so I nodded. I was partly happy that I was returning home, and partly sad that I had to leave Elkloria. There was so much to explore here, and so much to learn! But at that moment, I longed for my parents on Earth.

I quickly finished my food. Metara and Max got up after I was done, and Max murmured a spell. I felt like my clothes were vibrating. He murmured another spell, and we appeared at the entrance to the kingdom in Layer Vintilo. Marco waved at us.

Metara waved back. "Hey, Marco."

"Hello, Lady Metara. You are leaving the kingdom today?"

Metara smiled. "Yes. Princcens Khioneus wants to go to his home in Vhestibulium."

Marco nodded. "Of course, my lady."

Metara, Max, and I walked out of the hallway to the archway with the shifting lavender-tinged mist. We walked through and returned to those pixie-filled gardens.

Max cast another teleportation spell and brought us to the forest where I'd first come to Elkloria. The dark sphere flanked by Grecian columns stood in front of us. I walked up to the portal and suddenly realized Metara and Max weren't following. They looked tense.

"Something's not right," said Max.

"Everything seems alright to me. Come on. The portal's open, Mom and Dad are waiting, it's winter break—"

"Shut up!" snapped Metara. I looked at her in shock.

"I hear it," said Max softly.

"What?" I asked.

"The forest is too quiet."

"It is?" I couldn't hear anything. Oh, wait. That was the point.

An instant later, the black serpent smoked out of the portal. Max tackled me to the side, and the serpent's tongue lashed out and grabbed him instead. It dragged Max into its mouth, but right before he disappeared, he cast a spell. A swirling, purple vortex appeared beneath us, and we fell into a void of purple mist and lightning.

CHAPTER 5

Darkness and Magic

METARA AND I FELL OUT OF the vortex onto a bed of flowers. Several pixies buzzed away from us in surprise.

I jumped up. "Max! What happened? Where's Triskén? Where's Max?"

Metara's eyes were wide. "Triskén! It . . . "

"He's . . . he's not *dead*, is he?" I covered my mouth. Tears sprang to my eyes.

Metara shook her head. "Triskén captured him—the snake used its tongue to grab him, not kill him. It wants him for something."

I wiped my eyes. "We have to get him back. This is my fault."

Metara shook her head. "Max knew what he was doing. He put himself in harm's way, to save you."

"Why?"

"Max knows more magic than you. Letting himself be captured instead of you was smart. Let's talk to Nessa. She has a lot of power—political and magical. Whatever Triskén is doing, it's gotta be stopped. Besides, Max is Nessa's friend. She'll want to get him back."

Metara held her hands one above the other with both palms facing inward and murmured, "**Escubarum Elokium**." A glowing orb appeared between her hands. She closed her eyes. The glowing orb floated around her hands, trailing rainbow sparkles behind it.

The orb flashed red, and black spots flickered on it. The rainbow trail darkened. Then both the orb and the rainbow trail faded away.

Metara sighed. "The spell won't work. Wherever Max is, it's sealed to locator magic."

Metara banged on the apparently non-sentient doors of the throne room of Neurazia until Nessa opened them. Her smile disappeared when she saw our stricken expressions.

"Where's Max?" she asked.

Neither of us answered.

"Tell me everything," she said, walking to the dais.

When we were finished explaining, Nessa sat down on the dais and rubbed one hand over her eyes. "I'll talk to the NOTT. We'll form a rescue mission to Grimlochia . . . or wherever he's being held. Did you do a locator spell?"

Metara nodded. "Wherever Max is, I couldn't find him."

THE DOOR TO INFERNA

Nessa nodded. "I need to put the facts together with the Neurazian defense committee."

"I'll go right away." Metara vanished with a sucking sound, as if the air was rushing in to fill the vacuum she left behind.

"How long will that take?" I asked. "We don't know what Triskén will do to Max! I want to help! How can I help?"

"By staying safe and learning history," she said. "Triskén compromised the portal so we can't send you home. We'll keep you in the kingdom."

Anger surged through me. "Max is one of my best friends! I need to do something, not take a stupid history class!"

"It's not like you want him back more than the rest of us. He's my friend, too," Nessa said hotly. I winced. I hadn't meant it that way, though . . . I didn't know how I *had* meant it.

Nessa sighed. "We both need to calm down. I think I'm going to go to my room and upgrade my teleporter. You know what? Let's start your magical education. I'll talk to my friend Lianaka. She's a *phenomenal* history teacher."

"Seriously? I told you, I don't want to learn *history* while Max is in danger!"

Nessa gave me a sharp look. "History is important. Without it, you won't know anything about this world or its dangers. I'm not talking about boring history like whichever general united the lower regions of Elkloria. I mean the history of Triskén, the demons, magic—everything that relates to Max's current predicament. You want to help Neurazia and find Max? That's where you *start!*"

I gave a frustrated sigh. It was hard to argue with her logic. I *did* need to learn about Triskén. But . . .

Nessa held something out for me—a gold necklace with a blue stone pendant.

Seeing my face, she said, "Lia will teach you at the Temple of Psymus, because it's easier to focus your mind there. You're the youngest prince of the central royal bloodline. Your purple eyes are a dead giveaway. This will disguise them. Many times, the color of a wizard's eyes is believed to be their elemental alignment, excluding their kingdom's magic; a Neurazian wizard with red eyes may be believed to have a bit more powerful fire magic than other Neurazian mages. Purple eyes mean higher mind affinity, a characteristic of the royal family of Neurazia."

"Why don't you want me to attract attention?" I asked.

Nessa snorted. "Go without the amulet. There are a lot of fans of the 'long lost prince.' If you want to get torn to pieces by a horde of them, be my guest."

"Um . . . I'll take the amulet."

Nessa gave me a tense sort of smile. "Now, you need a history lesson. Let me tell you, Lia is the best history teacher *ever,* and she can divine like no one else. I'll show you to her room."

I frowned. What did she mean "divine like no one else?" Didn't that mean seeing the future or something?

Nessa took me through the maze of hallways in the palace to Lia's room. Then she turned around and left.

"Wait, Nessa, you can't just leave me! Couldn't you, like, introduce me to your friend?"

But she was already gone. I turned to the door, and said, "Uh, hello?"

A girl's face appeared in the door the way Enrique did. "Hello. I'm Carmen. Who are you?"

"I'm Khi. Nessa . . . I mean, Princess Khyonessa told me to meet Lianaka and have her take me to the Temple of Psymus?"

Carmen's eyes widened. "Oh, you're the prince! Okay, well, Lia's changing right now, she'll be out in a few minutes."

I nodded and waited until the door opened. Behind it was the girl with straw blonde hair who had greeted me when I first came to Palace Imagicetra.

"Hello, I'm Lianaka, but you can call me Lia. You're Princcens Khi, right?" She made the same gesture that she had performed when we first met—one hand out and the other at her collarbone. Then she beckoned. "Come. Let's go to the temple." She suddenly tensed, frowning, and put her hand on my forehead as if checking my temperature. "You're feeling a lot of worry. And some sadness. And fear. Why?"

"What did you do?" I asked, stupidly trying to look at her hand on my forehead.

"Empathic divination. What are you worried about?"

"My best friend, Max, was kidnapped by Triskén."

Lia's face filled with sympathy. "I'm sorry. I know him. I hope they rescue him."

Surprisingly, her words soothed me a little. "Thanks." There was something in her voice that reminded me of Metara's.

She guided me down the palace halls and into the garden, toward the silver building which housed the tube that led to the other layers. The tube didn't seem to continue upward, which I hadn't noticed before. If the palace was at the lowest layer, shouldn't the tube have led upward?

After a short and somewhat scary tube journey *downward*, we found ourselves in front of the temple. Beyond a small veranda, the temple was large and gray, with geometric carvings moving all over it (squares became circles, which became rhombi, and so on).

She guided me inside to a large statue of a slender man wearing a tunic covered in more geometric designs. He had three eyes, and his hand was touching a necklace at his throat that depicted a symbol of an eye.

Lia gestured to the statue. "This is Psymus, the god of the Mind."

I asked quietly, "Uh, why is no one, like, praying at the temple? I mean, it's a temple, right?"

Lia shrugged. "The common belief in Neurazia—the Ecclesia of Acutorias—is that the gods don't intervene with mortal lives. There are people who believe in devotion to the gods—the Ecclesia of Pictura—but they worship Psymus at five of-the-clock post meridiem. Nobody comes to pray in the early hours."

"Wait, so these gods . . . they actually exist?" I was skeptical.

Lia gave me a confused look. "Of course they do. Some powerful magics call on the power of the gods."

I glared at the statue of Psymus. If gods existed, why didn't they do anything to help Max?

For the next hour, Lia explained all sorts of things about Elkloria, drawing diagrams in the air with a magic pen.

There were these all-powerful beings, more powerful even than the gods Elklorians believed in, called Fae and demons, that were complete enemies. The Fae were beings whose existence was unconfirmed but assumed based off of heavy evidence in order to fill in the blanks of modern research to progress magical science (sort of like dark matter in Earth science), but everyone knew about demons—most people believed demons were the enemies of the gods, not the Fae.

Long ago, in a war before time, the Fae imprisoned the demons on a distant planet called Inferna. There was no way out except one. Strangely, the Fae had created a powerful portal that allowed minor demons to enter

Pyrhithya. The all-powerful, immortal ones couldn't get through.

No one knew why the Fae (or gods or cosmic forces or whatever) created this portal. Some speculated that the portal solved a magical imbalance. Others suspected it was a test by the Fae, a temptation of power, so the Fae could observe the greed of sentient living things like humans. Still others thought that it was because the ecosystems of Pyrhithya relied on the ecosystems of Inferna in some way.

The portal on the Elklorian side was surrounded by a huge wasteland continent on the other side of the ocean—the only other known continent on the planet. It was called the Wildlandes. The ocean between kept demons from traveling to Elkloria, because saltwater harmed demons and prevented teleportation. The wasteland was filled with so much dark magic that even the gods (and possibly the Fae) couldn't see inside the continent. The Wildlandes were a strange place, caught between two worlds and containing properties of both.

Lia began explaining Triskén's history, beginning with a kingdom of technological magic called Advanutiva. Advanutiva made many magitechnological advancements, but some of their inventions were tedious to reproduce. Forty years ago, they tried to make something that would locate and destroy darkness, calling it Kogiskén, meaning *finder of darkness*. However, the machine used a little dark magic, and something went wrong in one of the tedious parts of the machine. Maybe they just poured in two milliliters too much water—no one knew what the mistake had been.

So, like something out of a dystopian sci-fi story, Kogiskén became Triskén, the *creator* of darkness. It was a sentient dark entity, not truly alive but with dark magic so powerful that it was feared throughout the ten kingdoms of Elkloria—even throughout the four supernatural kingdoms of the ethereal gods, the chthonic gods, the Time Keepers, and the angels. Triskén corrupted the kingdom of Advanutiva, turning it into Grimlochia, the kingdom of darkness. Lia also mentioned that Advanutivan magic had filtered into Neurazian magic, so a few people had special Advanutivan spells or rare abilities, like Nessa's power of Invention. Supposedly, Nessa could mentally invent devices, like her teleporter, and bring them to "life" with her magic.

Triskén was hard to predict; no one knew his motives or intentions, only that it likely had something to do with the demons, the primal powers of darkness.

Why can't the gods just fix all this for us? I thought. Or *the Fae? If they were real and so powerful, why didn't they do anything?*

I learned that Phantasian was the language of magic, or whatever created magic. Many scholars believed that Phantasian was the Fae's language, named after Phantasia, the theoretical place where the Fae lived. Phantasian was also the cultural language of Elkloria. Like, Khioneus and Khyonessa were different ways to say *blizzard*, and Lianaka's name meant *lotus*. Names were generally Phantasian and Raviluxish, because those were the languages of the gods and magic, and people once believed such names would give them a heavenly mandate or something. People thought that naming their child something special would make the child special.

Like, Max's name, Maximillis, meant *charity* or *generosity*. Max cared more about others than about himself, so much so that he got captured because of me. Maybe the gods did exist . . . and were evil.

Nessa was right. The history lesson had helped. I now knew the basics of this world. Maybe I could be of use to the Neurazian defense committee or whatever. Okay, honestly, I probably wouldn't be of much use, but I planned on joining this committee and finding out exactly what I could do to help, no matter how little it was. I didn't care how limited my knowledge was. Max was most important.

CHAPTER 6

Science of Magic

AT BREAKFAST THE NEXT DAY, NESSA said, "We'll start your magic training today. I'll teach you offensive and defensive magic, Metara will teach restoration, and Lia will teach you illusion and mind magic. I'll take you to Hall Ofensia, but after that, you must find Hall Remenda and the Royal Library on your own. Come on."

"Wait," I said. "Any progress on Max?"

Nessa shook her head, her eyes downcast. "No. But it's . . . being handled, Khi. Don't worry. Max will be back safe and sound before you know it."

"I need to help," I mumbled, "I can't live with myself if I don't do *something*. He was trying to protect me."

"That's why we're starting your magic training," said Nessa. "So, you *can* do something."

She grabbed her teleporter and took my hand. She pressed a few buttons as we jumped, and we suddenly appeared in front of a door. A face appeared with blank eyes, angular features, and a straight mouth that showed no emotion whatsoever.

"Full name," it said in an electronic voice.

"Khyonessa Nevula," said Nessa.

"Please present your iris for the phorthel scanner," said the voice.

A beam of electric blue light shot out of the face's right eye and scanned Nessa's iris.

"Please present your thumb for scanning."

Nessa did just that, and the same electric blue light scanned her thumb.

The door opened, and Nessa walked into strange, swirling colors beyond it, beckoning me to follow her. As I walked into what was presumably some kind of portal, I bumped into something, and green sparks flashed across the air in front of me. The blank face appeared again. "New presence detected. Would you like to be validated?"

"Um, yes?" I said.

"Your full name?"

"Khioneus C—"

"Name accepted," it interrupted. "Please remove all your clothes so we can perform a phorthel—"

"Okay, override procedure, I authorize his access to the room," said Nessa.

The face bobbed as if it was nodding. "You are sure you want to override?"

Nessa nodded. "Yup!"

The face bobbed again. "Overridden. You now have access to the Armamentarium, Kee-oh-ness-ah and Kee-oh-knee-us-ess."

"It pronounced our names wrong," I said, frowning.

"Phantasian pronunciation. Though the 'ess' at the end of your name was probably because you started saying your middle name."

The face melted into the door, and we walked into the portal. A tingly feeling swooped over my skin. The room was dark, but a few shafts of light illuminated the floor.

I frowned at Nessa. "What was that all about?"

"For security scans, Elklorians use phorthel, which is Aethelum-enhanced light. It can scan anything—magic aurae, patterns, ionic waves, atom configuration . . . Phorthel is nearly foolproof, though it doesn't seem able to scan *through* things like clothes—"

"Not that! The whole security check! Why is that needed?"

"We are entering the Hall Ofensia. This is where the Neurazian security forces keep their weapons, so the security check keeps out bad people." She muttered something and light flared from orbs floating near the ceiling.

I looked around in shock. The walls were hanging with weapons. Guns, swords, ropes, gloves, more than I could take in.

Nessa snapped her fingers. "All right! Time to start basic spell training. We will go over the basic attack spell: Ofensia, like the name of this hall. Magic can be cast from pretty much any part of your body that has some kind of orifice or doesn't have too much hair—mouth, eyes, palms, elbows, etc. Magic comes out of your bloodstream through your flesh as a liquid known as Light Aethelum and vaporizes, triggering a spell. A spell is like a powerful force locked behind a door, and the words of the spell are the key that releases it. To trigger a spell, you simply say the trigger phrase, even though the main part of the casting is in your mind."

I thought back to when I had cast the spell that transformed my room. Enrique had said something similar about focusing on the outcome and saying the spell.

"Your magic is your life force, however," continued Nessa. "The more magic you use, the more fatigue you will feel. Your health will begin to deteriorate, causing sickness, bleeding, and even burns from 'glitching' magic. If the magic in your bloodstream becomes too low, you fall unconscious, and if it runs out, you die. Enchantments, like the MES enchantment you cast on your room, also wear off after a while, once your subconscious mind disconnects you from the enchantment to preserve your life force."

I thought about the spell—*enchantment*—I had cast on my room. How much magic had that used? Did I risk my life by casting it? Had my room already reverted to normal because of the life-force-preservation thing Nessa was talking about? What would happen to the stuff in the room when it reverted? Were the clothes that I left on the floor of the room gone forever or something? Not that it was a big deal. Wait. My phone was on the dresser. . .

"When you use magic to attack other creatures, it will directly attack their life force. And the huge rule of magic: you can't directly harm a being with your magic— unless that being has used magic to purposely kill or mortally wound someone. That's a different story then; their magic becomes polluted into what is known as Dark Aethelum, making them a dark creature and able to be killed by magic. Scientists attribute this change to a substance they call Karma, which has mass but does not seem to be matter. If you accidentally use a spell that would harm a being, they will be protected with a sort of temporary shield. It's inferred that this protection is caused by Karma. If you *intend* to harm them and kill them, the shield does not manifest, the being dies, and you become a dark wizard."

I nodded. "So, I couldn't harm you with magic unless I intended to, and then I would become a dark wizard?"

"Yup."

"But Triskén *can* kill Max because of its dark magic."

Nessa winced. "Well, yes. But it didn't. It captured him instead. Triskén has some other purpose for him."

"That doesn't really make me feel better."

Nessa sighed. "You're trying to make both of us feel bad."

"I . . . I'm sorry. What was that spell again?"

"Ofensia. Try it. Concentrate on what you want to happen. Imagine light pooling into your palm."

I closed my eyes, held my hand out, and imagined that something was traveling down my arm and out of my hand. "Ofenzia!"

Nothing happened.

Nessa whacked my head. "You pronounced it wrong, dummy! Oh-fen-SEE-ah!"

"Ofensia!"

Nothing happened.

Nessa tapped my head. "Concentrate!"

"Ofens—Ow! What was that for?" I rubbed my head where Nessa had whacked me yet again.

"It's not OFF-en-see-ah. It's OH-fen-see-ah!"

"Oh-fen-see-ah!"

"Faster!"

"Jeez! *Ofensia!*"

My hand glowed. It felt wet and warm at the same time. I yelped and tried to shake the feeling away. A beam of light shot out, hit a high window, and disappeared. The window remained unblemished and uncracked. I guess with all the security, the window was probably reinforced or something. Nessa snorted. With an affectionate smile she said, "You can't even aim properly! You're so incompetent."

I sighed. "I'm sorry. Where I come from, sparking hands are a *bad* thing."

Nessa shrugged. "All right, I believe you, but do the next spell properly. The next two are a little harder. They're called Fulminum and Heliolumina Magna. They both do different things and are the three basic offensive spells every Neurazian wizard learns. Fulminum creates an arc of magic electricity, and Heliolumina Magna creates fiery sunlight that magibyrnes dark creatures."

"Magibyrnes?"

"Burns by using potent light magic to create a reaction with dark magic—the two magics annihilate each other and create a burst of heat. How about we try Heliolumina Magna first?"

"Sure," I said.

Nessa shrugged. "You know the deal now. Stop talking and start doing!"

This time it only took two tries to get a beam of brilliant light sizzling into the wall. Then, I tried the Fulminum spell, creating an arc of electricity after three tries.

Nessa grinned. "Great! Now for defense. The spell is Shielt Fisicus. I'll shoot at you, and you use the spell to block it."

"Wait, what?"

Nessa grabbed a super sci-fi gun from the wall with a cyan tank on top. She aimed it at me and pulled the trigger. A glowing cyan sphere shot out right at my face.

"Ah!" I cried. **Shielt Fisicus!**"

The air in front of me rippled, and the blue sphere crashed into solid air, exploding in a burst of blue light. I was fine. The shield had worked!

Nessa grinned. "Well executed."

She was crazy. "You could have killed me!"

She smirked. "The phorthelsinphos blaster only disintegrates non-biological objects. The worst that would have happened is your clothes would have been vaporized. It wouldn't harm you."

My gaze was baleful. "You could have *told* me!"

"Then you wouldn't have been scared. Defensive magic works better on adrenaline. Now, I wanna show you something. This is *my* magic. I don't know why I can do this, but it's a powerful utility to me and all of Neurazia."

She closed her eyes and chanted something. Fire appeared in the air. I yelped and jumped back against the door. Shards of ice swirled around her, and music sounded—joyous music that sang of adventure. Flowers grew from the floor. Animals leapt from the shadows, dancing in rows and circles. Petals floated through the air and came together to create a picture of a face—my face. Hair formed from the ice (incorrectly colored, but pretty realistic). The face smiled, and even my dimples appeared on its cheeks.

My mouth dropped open. "Nessa . . . that's awesome."

She grinned. "You're not . . . surprised?"

"About what?"

"The fact I can use any magic. Which most people can't do."

"Wait, you mean I can't do what you did?"

Nessa suddenly yawned, probably tired from her magic casting. "Yes . . . I guess I never told you that wizards can only use spells from their own kingdom and the universal spells like Ofensia. I guess it's not important at the moment. Go to your next class."

I turned back to the door, feeling like I had disappointed Nessa somehow. "Uh, Hall Remenda?"

The blank face appeared. "Executing teleportation sequence. Please wait." The door opened and I walked into Hall Remenda. The room was quite big. It had tons of shelves and tables with big jars labeled things like Spiritine oak sap, Phlegethonian water, and Eldjotun's starfire petals. Kitchen tools hung from the walls. The main attraction was a huge empty cauldron in the center, set into the ground and surrounded by railings. There were pipes above it and levers along one wall that seemed connected to the pipes. It looked like a combination of a witch's potions room and a giant chemistry lab.

The door behind me hissed open, and Metara walked in. She smiled. "Good, you're early."

Metara taught me a spell called Fulminum Diem, which allowed me to consume lightning and electricity as if it were food. She also taught me a spell called Mendeala which could fix broken objects or heal skin wounds, which was quite tough, because you had to focus on many things at once. Metara showed me how to brew a potion that would cleanse dark magic wounds—like those inflicted by Triskén. In Vhestibulium, she had always studied biology and said she wanted to be a doctor. Apparently, she also wanted to be a magical healer in Elkloria.

According to Metara, if Max had been there, he would have taught me how to do "sorcery": magic not related to battle—conjuring food and decorations, duplicating things, transforming pumpkins into carriages, creating magical lockers, etc.

Sorcery sounded like fun. I wished Max had been there to teach me.

After Metara's class I met Lianaka again, Nessa's friend with straw blonde hair who had taught me about Fae and demons.

This time, she taught me Phantasian, the language of the Fae. It was older than all the languages that existed, and it filtered into many languages on Earth. She mostly taught me greetings and such. She taught me little tidbits of knowledge, like how mirrors can reflect or absorb dark magic, depending on how they're used.

Then Lia began teaching me the most complex magic I had learned so far—illusion spells like the one Metara had used to make a cheeseburger appear in my hand. You can simulate sight, sound, and smell, but not taste or touch. To simulate touch, you'd need to use shield spells.

As for taste . . . Lia said there was a spell, but it required mastery over lesser spells, a very particular state of mind, and fluent pronunciation. It struck me as kind of backwards that the spell I used to redesign my bedroom was less complex than a spell to simulate taste.

CHAPTER 7

NOTT

I LAY IN MY BED THAT night, in my still-existent MES, and looked at my phone. There was no internet, but I read a book I had downloaded from home. The door opened, and Nessa walked inside.

I put my phone on the dresser. "Enrique, I told you to keep her out!"

Enrique didn't answer. Ugh. What was with him? Had Nessa done something to him?

Nessa rolled her eyes. "I'm just checking on you."

"Any updates on Max?"

"No."

"What is that Neurazian defense committee doing?"

"We're investigating something. The Wildlandes has been surrounded by a fire storm called the Ignicastrum for a couple of months. We believe the darkins conjured it."

"Darkins?" I asked.

"The dark wizards of Grimlochia, corrupted by Triskén."

"Oh, right," I said.

She muttered a spell, and a glowing, milky white orb appeared in her hand. I touched it, and light exploded in my vision, then darkness. Suddenly, I was in a low-ceilinged wooden room with a table in the middle. The ground swayed, and I realized I was on a ship in some kind of cabin. A bunch of people I didn't know sat around the table. I tried to move closer, but I couldn't move a muscle. I couldn't even blink.

A silver-haired man stood up. He was tall, thin, and didn't look that old despite his hair—then again, in Elkloria, a person's hair color could be any color from iridescent green to fiery orange. Somehow, I knew his name was Sir Korukan and that he was the leader of the NOTT.

He said, "We'll scout the Wildlandes and try to find the source of the disturbance in the northern carva-cathonic field."

I turned and said, "I'm going outside." I didn't have control over what I was doing, and I realized I was Nessa, experiencing everything through her eyes.

Nessa ran out onto the deck. The sky rapidly turned orange, and a wall of fire blazed on the horizon—even on the waves themselves. The firestorm roared and roiled. Electric bolts flashed within it, and flames flared from its torrid orange surface.

"Where the vexing hex did that come from?" said Sir Korukan.

As the ship drew closer, the raging sea swelled, and an enormous head with horizontal-pupiled eyes surfaced and made an unearthly shriek. The beast had tentacles like an octopus, but the lump-shaped body that surfaced from the water had the beak of a bird. A huge tentacle shot toward the ship, knocking it about.

"It's a kraken," Nessa said in awe.

A second monstrous head emerged from the water. It was dark green and fishlike with purple eyes, fins, spindly teeth, and long whiskers like a catfish. Its mouth glowed red.

Someone shouted, "Leviathan!"

Green tentacles from the leviathan's serpentine body streaked around the ship's mast. More tentacles lashed around Nessa, who screamed and shot a fireball at the leviathan.

Nessa yelled, "Activate the transvallic field!"

Someone nearby looked at her wide-eyed. Nessa nodded firmly. He started chanting. The ship's hull glowed. As the chanter finished his recitation, a translucent field surrounded the ship, dotted with sparks of blue. The scenery outside the field changed from deadly monsters and a firestorm to a peaceful harbor. The tentacle around Nessa fell to the deck, severed and oozing blood.

"The monsters must be darkin tools to protect the Wildlandes," said Korukan. "What are they planning? Are they trying to open the demon portal?"

The scene blackened, and suddenly I was back in my room. Nessa's memory pearl disappeared. She looked at me expectantly.

"I don't care what they're planning," I said. "I want to save Max."

"The Neurazian Order of Triskén's Termination, the NOTT, is the Neurazian defense committee," said Nessa. "It is a very specialized organization. You'd have to pass a test to enter it."

"How do I join? Can you test me?"

Nessa pressed her lips together. "If you want to join the NOTT, I'll need a strong reason to nominate you—you only know five spells. I know you want to get Max back, but that's not reason enough, no matter how much you care about him."

"All right." I thought for a second. What did I have to offer the NOTT? Suddenly, my vision went white. A voice echoed from somewhere, and with a shock, I realized it was mine:

"The holy one reveals,
The demon child conceals.
By the twins, the soul temple's key be obtained
To unlock the way to the land untamed.
Goddess of dark and soulless night,
Open the gate as Lunella loses sight.
Life of the loved one, key to the dark,
Eternal darkness, universal war.
Loved one's life for the gate to Sheol.
Complete the cycle for the savior of old."

I blinked rapidly and shook my head. "What the heck just happened?"

Nessa looked shocked. "I think you just said . . . a prophecy."

I stared at her. "A prophecy?"

She nodded. "Your eyes went all glowy, your hair whipped around your head, and you floated off the bed a little bit. Your voice was really weird, too, all echoey and deep. And what you said was definitely a riddle—prophecies are usually riddles."

"Cliché," I muttered. "Okay, why am I speaking *prophecies?*"

"Well, I hear that prophets are made when Destinis pours the nectar of fate into their mouths. Do you remember ever drinking the nectar of fate?"

"Um . . . no?"

"No, you obviously don't. Your prophecy indicates a strange turn of events."

She raised her eyebrows and tapped her chin. "We have to talk with the NOTT about this. Prophets are so rare. They're the mouthpieces of deities. But the future always changes. There's a rule of quantum physics that if you try to calculate the position of a particle, you can't calculate its speed, and if you try to calculate its speed, you can't calculate the position. But if you calculate both, you can calculate the future, and the future, like quanta, falls from a state of superposition into—"

"Speak English, please!"

"'English?' What's that?"

I'd forgotten. Elklorians called English "Common Tongue."

"Explain it to me as if I don't know anything about quantum physics except for the word *quantum.*"

"Oh! Basically, the god of fate, Destinis, has the power to see both sides of the . . . coin of fate, you could call it. He can observe the future. The unobserved future is pure potential—it is unwritten and can be anything. But occasionally, Destinis will tell a future he calculated using a prophet as his mouthpiece. Now that you, the mouthpiece of Destinis, spoke this future, the future's superposition has collapsed into one possibility—the only future that can possibly happen now. Your prophecy has become the fate of everything that exists. But its wording is flexible. We can't be sure of the exact meaning."

"I'm not liking this fate god very much—he's stuck us in a single path, a single future. Do I still have the power to make my own choices?"

Nessa shrugged. "Who knows? Fate's a funny thing. For better or worse, it sets us on a single path to prevent a crisis. If only Destinis sent us prophecies that were a little less ambiguous . . . "

I shrugged. "Still don't like this fate god guy, but . . . since I'm his mouthpiece, do I have deity powers now or something?"

"No, but the fact you are a prophet at all means something *big* will happen in the future—probably something bad. It's possible that you'll have a big part in it."

My face paled. "You're scaring me. That sounds like everything we've been afraid of, with Max captured and darkins and demonic lands and portals to demon worlds."

Nessa said, "Can you recall the prophecy?"

I frowned. "Um . . . "

Suddenly, the words of the prophecy tumbled out of my mouth again. Nessa rapidly wrote the words in the air with a magical pen.

"Wow," I said, when I was done. "That was . . . a weird experience."

Nessa laughed. "We should try to dissect the prophecy."

We both looked up at the words Nessa had written, floating in the air.

Nessa tapped her chin thoughtfully. "The first two lines—*the holy one reveals, the demon child conceals*—what could those mean?"

"They seem to be separate from the rest of the prophecy. They don't have much information. I'm more interested in the part that says *By the twins, the soul temple's key be obtained / To unlock the way to the land untamed.*"

"It sounds like it has something to do with a key to the Wildlandes," I said, "and the *twins* in the prophecy . . . are those *us*? *We* have to find this key?"

Nessa shrugged. "It's possible. It's *probable*. But the soul temple . . . not sure what that means."

I read out the next two lines:

"Goddess of dark and soulless night,
Open the gate as Lunella loses sight."

Nessa said, "Lunella is the moon god, so the day he loses his sight would be a lunar eclipse of the winter moon Nimori, a blood moon. That's the birth of Yesus!"

"What?" I asked.

"The day when Yesus Christus was born. Uh, I think Vhestibulians have a name for it, like Natchrist? Christnat?"

"Christmas?"

"Yes!" said Nessa. "That's in five days." A look of horror crept onto Nessa's face.

"That's bad, isn't it?" I asked.

"Most likely," said Nessa. "And who is the goddess of dark and soulless night? What is the *open the gate* part? What gate? Gate to what?" She scanned the prophecy intently, her eyes alighting on a sentence near the bottom.

"There's something about 'Sheol' down here," she muttered to herself. "What does that mean? Is that some place in the spirit world?"

"Um," I said. "I'm not going to ask what that is. But listen to this: *Life of the loved one, key to the dark, / Eternal darkness, universal war* . . . Oh no. Max is a loved one. I love him, Metara loves him, his parents love him. . . . And *key to the dark* sounds like some sort of sacrifice. In five days!"

Max's capture was bad enough, but Max being sacrificed in a *less than a week*? I didn't care if I knew only five spells. I had to join the NOTT and help save him.

Nessa's eyes widened. "Open the gate . . . key to the dark . . . universal war . . . I know what Sheol is! It's one of the names for Inferna, the demon world! The darkins are going to sacrifice Max to release the demons. We need to get to the NOTT right away."

"Yeah, we do!" I jumped out of bed and headed for the door.

Nessa's mouth twitched. "Um, Khi? Not that the NOTT has rules on formality, but . . . "

I looked down and realized I was in my silk, palatial nightclothes. "Oh. Right."

Nessa muttered a spell, and I was suddenly wearing robes. "You don't want to make a bad first impression. But I think you'll pass the test at least, being a prophet and all."

I shrugged. "I'm glad it was so easy."

Joining the NOTT might be dangerous. It might be throwing myself in a war between magical factions, trying to keep evil maleficent wizards from releasing the most powerful beings that existed. But for those I loved, I would do anything. That thought surprised me, but I knew it was true.

Nessa and I teleported from the hallway outside my room since the teleporter didn't work inside bedrooms. We appeared in front of a door in which a new face appeared.

"Oh, new people! I'm Rosaura, but you can call me Rosie!" The door's face seemed young, like a teenager.

She giggled and bombarded me with questions. "So, what's your name? Where are you from? How old are you? Are you single? What's your favorite color? Are you part of the royal family?"

Nessa stepped in. "Calm down, Rosie. This is my brother, Khi. He's fourteen and single, and his favorite color's blue, but Rosie—"

"Only fourteen?" Rosie said curiously. "He looks so much older."

Nessa said, "Yes, he's tall. Rosie, we have something important to tell Sir Korukan. Can you please let us through?"

Rosie giggled again. "'Course! I'll call him right away!" She opened to reveal a large, circular room lit by long glowing bars on the ceiling that looked like fluorescent lights. Long curved tables were set around the room with several chairs along their lengths and a desk in front of them. A glowing screen hung behind the desk. A large banner hung on one wall, depicting a circle with four arrowheads pointing outward and a pair of blank eyes in the center.

I followed Nessa to the large desk. After a couple of minutes, the door opened, and a tall, silver-haired man walked to the desk. I recognized him immediately as Sir Korukan.

"Hello, Princess Prissy—uh, Princcentassa Khyonessa," he said. Nessa rolled her eyes with a smile. "And hello to you, Princcens Khioneus! How have the both of you been?"

"Fine," said Nessa, as I said, "Terrible."

Nessa frowned at me and shrugged. "Well, okay, nothing's really been fine except for Khi coming home. He was attacked by Triskén, and then his best friend was kidnapped."

Sir Korukan nodded. "That's why I asked how you've been. But why are you here so late? It is nine and thirty of-the-clock. You should be in bed. Not that princesses have a curfew, but you do need your strength to serve the kingdom."

"Well . . . " Nessa turned to me. "Can you do it again, Khi?"

I wasn't sure. I thought about Grimlochia, Triskén, and Max. I tried to recall the prophecy, and suddenly I levitated slightly, my hair whipping around, my vision going white, and the prophecy spilled out of my mouth. When it was over, Sir Korukan looked at me in shock, and I felt my cheeks redden. Once again, Nessa had written out the prophecy in the air (or maybe she had done the magical equivalent of copy/paste).

"A prophecy," Korukan said. "About the Sheol—which, I'm sure you realized, is another name for Inferna. Cursed Noxoniata! The darkins' plan in the Wildlandes must be worse than we thought."

"We think we understand parts of it," said Nessa. "Lunella losing sight refers to the blood moon on the birth of Yesus five days from now, and the life of the loved one is Max's life, which is probably going to be sacrificed or something to open the demon portal. If we're right, we have less than a week! We have to save him!"

Korukan put his hands up. "Slow down. We have to try to understand the other parts of the prophecy as well." He turned to the glowing words in the air.

"The holy one reveals, the demon child conceals . . . Well, there are many 'holy ones' and 'demon children' in Elkloria, so that part is unclear, but it says the 'demon child *conceals,* which could mean that someone demonic is among us . . . "

"But demonic doesn't mean evil," said Nessa. "Remember that recruit named Furorde? He had a demonic amulet that gave him power, but his heart was right, and he used it for good. Furorde may have a part to play in this prophecy."

"You're right," said Korukan. "One's magic does not determine their allegiance. The 'holy one' could also be evil for all we know."

I rubbed my temples. "I don't understand why we're talking about this. We should focus on the important parts, like saving Max and stopping the demons from coming out of Inferna."

"Yes," said Korukan. "Okay, so eternal darkness and universal war means the release of the demons. *Life of the loved one key to the dark . . .* You think that means Younger Lord Max shall be sacrificed to open the demon portal? The *dark* can refer to many things."

I pointed at the words in the air. "It says Sheol by name, and Max *is* a loved one to many of us, *and* he was captured by Triskén for some dark purpose."

I forced myself to breathe. "I don't want him to die."

"No one does," said Korukan, laying his hand on my shoulder. His eyes were melancholy. "Younger Lord Max's life is precious. And you're right, it does seem that Triskén intends to sacrifice Max to release the most powerful evil creatures in existence."

"It also says the loved one's life for the gate to Sheol," said Nessa. "What does that mean?"

"So, the first time the words *loved one* appear is in *life of the loved one key to the dark*," said Korukan. "There is no verb, meaning it's possible the loved one isn't sacrificed to open the gate—though I'm not sure what it means for the loved one's life to be 'for' the gate of Sheol. The *life of the loved one* being *key to the dark* simply means that the loved one's life *can* be the key to the dark but doesn't *have* to be. Obviously, he could be *used* as the key, but it could be interpreted either way. Prophecies tend to be about technicalities in the wording."

"I don't like this at all," I muttered.

"Don't worry, Princcens. We will figure out something to save Max."

"Where do we start?" asked Nessa.

"The Temple of Azatalan in the Selebrassa Forest, where people honor the souls of the deceased," said Korukan. "I have a hunch that's what the prophecy refers to. We don't know what this 'key' looks like, but I have a feeling you'll know it when you see it—and I bet there will be heavy defenses around it."

Nessa's eyes widened a little. "I'm going right away. We don't have a lot of time."

She pulled out her teleporter. As she pressed the button, I grabbed her hand.

"Exception in T Linker," came an electronic voice. "Too much mass detected. Unable to teleport."

Nessa looked at me, confused. "What are you doing? I have to go!"

"Take me," I said. "The prophecy says *twins*, not *twin*."

Sir Korukan spoke up. "I also think Khi should go with you. His prophesying will probably be useful, and he knows a few offensive spells. Consider this his initiation into the NOTT."

Korukan turned to me. "Assuming he accepts, of course."

"Yes! I would love to join!" I exclaimed.

Korukan smirked. "You'll need your insignia and tools."

He took me to a dark room and flicked the light on. The room was full of tables cluttered with odd, golden pendants with aqua blue gems set in them.

Korukan took a glowing blue pen from one of the shelves. "Where do you want your insignia?"

I shrugged. I didn't know what he meant.

"I'll put the insignia on your shoulder."

He pulled down my collar to expose my shoulder and touched the pen to my deltoid. A blue symbol appeared on my skin—the same symbol on the banner outside, a circle with four arrows facing outward and a pair of eyes in the center. Korukan then grabbed a small, translucent sphere from a shelf. A hazy blue shape swirled in the center.

Korukan said the sphere was an amulet that allowed for secure communication spells—using communication channels that were very hard to "interize," the magical equivalent of hacking.

Nessa walked into the room and smiled at me. "Welcome to the Neurazian Order of Triskén's Termination, Khi."

CHAPTER 8

Azana

NESSA AND I TELEPORTED TO THE edge of a large forest. The dark green trees looked blue in the odd light of the moon: full and glowing a bright blue. The planet's translucent rainbow rings crossed it.

"Nimori will be a supermoon soon. This year, the Birth of Yesus will happen when the moon is both a supermoon and a blood moon," said Nessa.

The leafy ground was cast with a bright silvery glow. The leaves on the trees glittered like gems, though many of the trees were bare in the winter. Glowing mushrooms grew in the roots of trees, giving the forest an ethereal look. Magical. Which it was.

The forest was pretty but silent (if you don't count the sound of the wind blowing the tree branches). There were no animals. It felt ominous.

Nessa peered at some silvery blue stuff on a tree and frowned. "Ectoplasm," she muttered. "There are ghosts in this forest."

I'd thought it was just moonlight, but now I realized it was something different.

I turned to Nessa, afraid. "So paranormal stuff exists, too?"

"I assume you're talking about the field of magic and knowledge relating to the souls of the dead," said Nessa. "It's *properly* called 'paramundane.' When someone is killed by magic or is killed in a place saturated with magic, their soul inhabits the magic particles and turns them into an insubstantial being that cannot touch physical objects but can create things on a paramundane level, including enchantments, so that they can affect the physical world, slightly. That's what a ghost is."

I shivered. "So, uh, do you know how to, like, exorcise ghosts or . . . "

Nessa shook her head. "Exorcism is for killing or sending away spirits, not ghosts. A ghost's removal is called *extrusion.* You either have to avenge their death, complete their unfinished business, or convince them that their business is complete. They can see through magic illusions, however. It's possible to force them to leave our world, but it's painful for both the ghost and any humans around, including the caster, and it has negative effects on the environment. When the ghost is gone, they pass on to the afterlife, which scientists call Mortis."

The concept of scientific study of what happened after death was so alien. I never believed there was an afterlife, but here in Elkloria the idea of an afterlife seemed ridiculously logical.

"What if the ghost has *no* unfinished business?"

"Anyone who's murdered by magic will have unfinished business."

Nessa and I continued cautiously down a path that was on the forest floor which probably led to the temple. Nessa muttered, "**Transforma Calois Apradostus Visuus**." A glowing trail appeared on the forest path, meandering and disappearing into the surrounding bushes. Several glowing orbs appeared on the tree branches as well.

I turned to Nessa. "What did you do?"

"Ghosts leave behind ectoplasm. It's a type of oxidation, I guess. New ectoplasm, like the patch I saw before, can be seen with the naked eye, but for older patches, I have to use this ectomagical spell. Now we can see where the ghost went. All NOTTians can use paramundane magic because of an amulet—not the communication amulet—implanted in our tattoo."

"Implanted in me?"

Nessa shrugged. "Well, you gave consent to it."

It still seemed sort of creepy.

Nessa pointed at the ectoplasm. "There's a ton of ectoplasm and several defensive ghost enchantments. See those orbs? Something is harassing the ghost."

"Maybe it's whatever's guarding the key to the Wildlandes," I said.

Nessa nodded. "That's likely."

She grabbed my hand and pulled me down the path (she really doesn't let me do things on my own, does she? I'm perfectly capable of walking!), following the trail of ectoplasm. The trail followed the forest path until it reached a bluish wall made of shiny stones, with an archway that read "Temple of Azatalan" and "Temple of the Soul" underneath that. Nessa and I walked through the archway. I was suddenly feeling nervous about the ectoplasm. Horror movies always scared me. Who can stand to watch people get ripped limb from limb? Hopefully this trail didn't end in zombies.

Inside the temple were strange, dead gardens. A few dying leaves were tinged dark blue. The sky was filled with stratus clouds of the same dark blue hue that became redder as they got closer to the horizon, and the planet's rings were not visible. Tall towers were visible past the garden, surrounding a dark, domed building silhouetted against the horizon.

"Strange," Nessa said. "There doesn't seem to be any kind of holy energy. The Tieroaelk is all corrupted."

"Tieroaelk?" I asked.

"It's a holy temple stone, but its structure has been changed somehow. Can you smell the Dark Aethelum?"

"Dark Aethelum has a smell?"

"Yeah," said Nessa. "It's a putrid, garbage-like smell. You know, how Light Aethelum has a sweet smell?"

I did smell something that reminded of sugar back at the Palace Imagicetra. Was that the smell of *magic*?

"Come on," said Nessa. "We don't have—"

She stopped suddenly and turned back toward the archway. "Who's there? Show yourself! **Antapra Mortigen**!"

Nessa waved her hand and an apparition appeared in the archway—a blue-tinged, translucent girl. She wore a frilly dress covered in bows. Two fairy wings flapped behind her. Her eyes were dark holes, and she had no nose. Her face was expressionless.

"Oh God." I blanched.

Nessa sighed. "Take it off," she said to the ghost.

The ghost pulled her face off! My eyes widened. Underneath was the cheerful face of a ten-year-old girl. She tossed the mask aside, and it dissolved into the air.

"Hello, I'm Azana. You must be wizards. I'm a ghost!" She talked super fast, her voice reverberating.

"Hi . . . Azana," I said. "What are you doing here?"

Nessa gave me a sharp look, and I realized how mean that question might be to a ghost. Obviously, she was here because she'd been murdered by magic. Why didn't I think before speaking?

Her face became downcast, her voice no longer fast or energetic. "I died in the temple. Now I can't leave until I've been avenged. I came here to pay my respects to my parents. I'm an orphan. I was visiting the Pergola of Good Lives in the temple, but something was wrong. The Pergola's unicorn statue, the Entriqua hor Viviannis Benvola, wasn't there. The statue represents the fortunes of the deceased, and it has always been a symbol of goodness. As I walked to where the Entriqua had been, something moved in the shadows. Gold eyes glinted at me. Suddenly, the Entriqua appeared—it was alive! It raised its horn and shot a beam of darkness at me. I wish I could do something about the darkness of the temple, but . . . "

Nessa looked at me and softly said. "We didn't come here for this . . . "

"Right, but," I said, "we can't just abandon her."

Nessa sighed. "If a ghost wants something, the least forceful way to send it to the world of the dead is by finishing its business. I guess that means defeating the evil unicorn statue. If it's the key's guardian, then that aligns with our goal."

We stepped inside the dark building. We were in some kind of courtyard. Clouds swirled above, suffused with moonlight. We followed a raised path over more gardens.

We came to a sort of gazebo. Nebulous, smoky snakes of shadow floated within. As we drew closer, they turned to us. One howled at me like a wolf and slithered through the air toward me. Nessa chanted a long spell— somehow without stuttering. The air rippled. A shimmering draconian shape flew toward the snakes on heat-haze wings. It slashed at them, tearing them into smoky shreds. "We should look around for the key," said Nessa. "Look for anything that smells *really* bad, like it has a lot of dark magic."

I shrugged and looked around nervously. The gazebo was very clean. There weren't even rocks lying around. I looked around the pillars holding up the roof. Nothing.

Nessa frowned. "It could be concealed. Let's search the rest of the temple first, though."

We walked along the path, until we reached an archway that read "Pergola of Good Lives." Behind it was a round pergola with a statue of a dark unicorn. It was frozen in a rearing pose, with glinting red jewels for eyes. Its skin was smooth gray stone, darker than the temple's normal stone. A marble horn jutted from its head, glinting in the faint light from the swirling clouds.

Nessa and I moved to either side of the unicorn, on guard. That's when it neighed. It fell on all fours and faced me, but it didn't charge. Ten pillars of darkness glided around the unicorn from the shadows. Each had a strange mask in the center. Smoky tentacle arms emerged from the pillars, shooting serrated discs that spun at me in a silver blur. I ducked, but a beam of black light shot from the unicorn's horn and slammed into my chest. I gasped. Nessa screamed. My knees gave way.

Thankfully, the pain became a dull ache after a few seconds, and I gathered enough strength to shoot Heliolumina Magna twice from my hands. Two of the pillars dispersed into clouds then burned away. Nessa destroyed the other eight with more Heliolumina Magna spells and helped me to my feet. The unicorn galloped toward me. I tried to move, but pain flared in my chest and I collapsed. The unicorn ducked its head and its horn stabbed straight into my stomach.

CHAPTER 9

Triskén's Return

NESSA'S SCREAM WAS TERRIFYING, BUT SURPRISINGLY, there was no pain at all. The horn shattered. I wasn't dead. I wasn't even bleeding.

My stomach was fine—no holes or blood or anything.

The light in the unicorn's eyes dimmed, and its skin became white marble. The statue fell over, but it didn't shatter.

Nessa looked at me in shock then ran over to me. She pulled the front of my robe open and frantically inspected my unharmed stomach. "Are you hurt? By the supreme light goddess Paluxina's holy name, are you actually okay?"

"I'm fine. Don't worry. Please let go of my robe now."

Nessa was practically hyperventilating as she let go of my robe and I self-consciously buttoned it up. "Gods, how did you do that? You could have died. You *should* have died! The curse on the unicorn must have dissolved at the last minute and it just . . . By Noxoniata's cursed name, *never ever get in an evil unicorn's way ever again or I will murder you! You got that?* How the Inferna did you dissolve that curse?"

I shrugged. "Um . . . maybe I cast some sort of curse-breaking spell?"

"You never learned Maledictum Soliven, and that spell is only for tiny curses! And the unicorn's curse was *not* a tiny curse!"

I blinked. "Oh. Um. Well . . . you said I was the vessel of the fate god or whatever. Could the fate god have saved me?"

"Prophets aren't protected by gods. You're thinking of klerikoi, though they're protected by spirits and mystical entities, not gods. Prophets speak for the fate god, nothing else." She looked mystified.

"Well, is it possible I'm a kleri-whatever . . . ?" Being under the protection of a powerful being sounded pretty great.

She shook her head. "You'd have pupil-less eyes and all sorts of weird, glowing symbols on your body. I wonder if it's a special ability, one of those magic life-sequence mutations, like my omni-magic . . . "

She waved her speculations away. "It doesn't matter right now . . . Let's find the key, but don't split up. I don't want you to get hurt."

A breeze ruffled my hair and brought with it a nasty smell, like rotting meat, and I coughed, my eyes watering. My gaze fell on the tallest tower of the temple. Thick, black smoke swirled above it. The breeze seemed to be coming from that direction.

"I think I've found something," I said.

Nessa followed my gaze and wrinkled her nose. "Looks evil to me. And that smell! Ugh! Let's use the hoverboard spell, Levibordum. It's not very durable though, so don't go crashing into things."

I cast the spell (it took three tries, but it seems the great thing about magic is once you cast a spell success-fully, it's easy to do it again). I suddenly rose up on a flat oval made of a sparkling, glass-like cyan substance. Colors swirled inside the hoverboard, like paint in water.

We floated up to the tallest tower. As we came near the black mass, bolts of darkness shot out and hit our hover-boards. They shattered, and the force of the blast tossed us several hundred feet into the sky before our momentum petered out and we started falling.

I screamed. I couldn't die like this, without seeing Max safe or—A gust of magical wind caught us, and we floated down toward the roof of the tower. Nessa. At least she had kept her head at terminal velocity. My heart was still racing.

As we descended on the cushion of air, a hissing voice came from the depths of the darkness. It sent chills down my spine, and I worried about this mission. But I knew, if

I ever wanted to save Max, I had to face this darkness—
Triskén's darkness. My resolve strengthened.

I saw movement in the darkness and glowing purple
eyes. Dark, nebulous purple chains wrapped around me,
cold against my skin. I struggled to break free. The chains
slowly tightened.

A hissing voice came from the mass. "The chains of
self-control. Break them, and your magic will fail when it
is most needed."

"What does that mean?" I said.

Chains of self-control? Magic would fail me? What did
that mean?

I gasped for air and felt panicked as I realized the
chains were suffocating me. I remembered the curse
breaking spell Nessa mentioned. I doubted I could get it
first try, but what other option did I have?

"**Maledictum Soliven!**"

White light sliced through the chains, and they vaporized. I was surprised. I thought the chains would be
stronger than that. Triskén had said that thing about the
chains of self-control, and I nervously wondered whether
breaking those chains had consequences. Well . . . at least
I hadn't asphyxiated?

"**Ofensia,**" I said. Projectiles shot from my hand at
Triskén, this time made of the same stuff as the hoverboard instead of a beam of light.

The projectiles went right through the darkness. No
physical attacks, then . . . but my magic *was* working. Did

that mean Triskén had lied about how my magic would fail me? Or was it more complicated?

Nessa shot a spell of scalding sunlight at it, but Triskén's gaseous form dispersed around it and came back together. Nessa said that was a powerful spell made to combat darkness, but nothing was working on Triskén.

A skin-crawling laugh echoed out of the darkness. "You won't defeat me. End this futile quest."

Nessa glared at Triskén. "Shut up! You kidnapped Max and want to destroy the world! We are not giving up."

Nessa turned to me, and her voice suddenly echoing in my head startled me. *I'm going to tell you a spell I once made. Use it on Triskén! I can't!* She then proceeded to telepathically tell me a long spell.

Why can't you do it? I thought really hard, hoping she could hear me.

That doesn't matter! Use the spell! Her voice in my head sounded angry and panicked. Why couldn't she cast the spell? Had something happened to her?

Nessa recited the spell in my head, and I said it out loud along with her. Small spheres of light appeared around Triskén. They pulsed, and beams of light shot from them, piercing Triskén's dark essence. But once again, the spells didn't harm it. An angry heat radiated from Triskén. Nessa said, "**Fuigna Drakonai**," and gold fire spilled from her mouth, burning a hole into Triskén's darkness. But the darkness was not clear for long before Triskén shot two dark tentacles at us, snaking erratically through the air. They wrapped around us, and we found ourselves in another place—gray sky and dark grass extending endlessly into the horizon.

I turned to Nessa. "Where are we?"

She gritted her teeth and squeezed her eyes shut, veins pulsing in her forehead. Suddenly, the world shattered—the gray sky and dark grass breaking into shards and falling away. We were back at the temple. The black tentacles were still around us, pulling us toward Triskén's dark mass. Nessa said something, and flashes of light broke the shadows around me. I tumbled backward.

Nessa stood next to Triskén's body mass, darkness spilling out of it and coalescing into the form of a fanged woman. She was beautiful like an explosion—a horrible, ominous kind of beautiful. She had gray skin, dark hair, and a black dress with a ragged hem. Her face was the same one I had seen in the darkness of the moon so long ago—a few days ago, actually, though it felt like it had been a year—when I had been on Earth and hadn't known a thing about Elkloria.

She transformed again into three enormous serpents. Their heads swayed as they hissed at us. One lunged at me, its long, curved fangs prepared to pierce into my skin, but I jumped out of the way just in time.

Two dark tentacles shot out of the dark mass that still floated behind the snakes. One latched onto Nessa. I barely dodged the other. Nessa fought for breath as it constricted her. The tentacles pulsated with light and she made a choking sound.

"Nessa!" I cried.

Triskén—reforming the face of that creepy woman—turned to me. "She cannot speak spells now. The tentacles prevent her vocal apparatus from vibrating. I will kill her, Khioneus—your dear sister, whom you have grown to love despite not knowing her for most of your life. You cannot save her now. Your magic cannot help you. When you broke my dark chains, you contracted yourself to being unable to harm me. Remember? The chains of self-control? A contract spell. You are not powerful enough to do anything for her, and the contract prevents you from doing anything anyway. I will make you an offer, Khioneus. I will free her and your friend, Maximillis, and I will stop attacking the Elklorian kingdoms if you send the Elklorians a message. Tell them to help me in my plans."

"But . . . don't you need Max to open the portal?" I asked.

"With the cooperation of the Elklorians, there are far easier ways to get to my goal. I'm willing to give up Max for that. It is a fair trade. Do you know, people of your world are so . . . selfish. They follow their own desires without regard for others' well-being. They start petty wars for land or public image, and many die because of it. But the demons . . . they can fix all of it. They will destroy and recreate both worlds perfectly, as utopias. I am saving the universes. If you try to stop me, you will be the real villain. Besides, you know the consequences if you don't cooperate." She waved a hand at Nessa.

The demons . . . trying to fix the world. Could they though? Could they actually fix the problems plaguing Earth—war, famine, global warming?

Did it matter? Triskén had kidnapped Max in order to sacrifice him for that perfect world. Why on Earth—or Pyrhithya for that matter—would I join such a horrible entity? Triskén didn't even have a human mind! It was like an AI with no conscience.

But . . . how could I distract Triskén and save Nessa?

Desperately, I said, "Triskén! If you release Nessa, I'll give you a prophecy! I'm a prophet!"

Nessa's eyes widened, and she shook her head.

Triskén tilted its head and smiled. "I knew you were a prophet . . . but I admit, I am intrigued."

I didn't know how I was going to do it. How did the last prophecy happen? I had thought of a question, and the prophecy, it seemed, gave me an answer. "Give me Nessa. Then I'll give you a prophecy."

Triskén smiled, shark-like. "How do I know you'll keep your word? How do I know Khyonessa won't attack me once I release her? She is a very powerful wizard."

"I guess you don't. But I have more to lose, and you can tell I'm not really a threat. Nessa's more powerful— you could give her to me . . . unconscious, so she doesn't cast magic." I winced as I said it—not only because I suggested Triskén knock Nessa unconscious but also because I was promising something I might not be able to give.

Triskén shrugged. "Have it your way." A tentacle of darkness creeped over Nessa's nose, and Nessa slumped. For a second I was frozen, worried Triskén had just killed Nessa, but I saw her breathing.

Nessa dropped to Triskén's feet. I approached slowly, keeping my eyes on Triskén. I knelt down and lifted Nessa. She was shockingly light.

"Prophecy, please," said Triskén.

"Okay," I said. "Give me a question to answer."

Triskén raised its eyebrows. "Do I win?"

I focused on the question. No prophecy came. "Uh . . . I think I need a more specific question?"

Triskén rolled its eyes. "All right. Do I open the demon portal?"

Again, I focused. Again, nothing came. "Give me a sec," I said, panicking. The first time I spoke a prophecy was when I tried to come up with ideas to reach the Wildlandes. The prophecy had only acted as a supplement, it seemed. It probably only came when I wasn't looking for information. Great. It would probably never happen again.

Okay, what about my old prophecy? I could remember it clearly.

"Life of the loved one, key to the dark, eternal darkness, universal war," I said. The wording could suggest the portal might open or not. Hopefully, Triskén interpreted it as the former and left us alone.

Triskén tilted its head. "What happened to the glowing eyes, levitation, and blowing hair?"

"Um . . . that was a prophecy I already had before," I said nervously. "I repeated it."

Triskén flicked its hair. "My magic tells me you're not lying, but you're not telling me the entire truth either. I'm impressed. Quite deceptive. You just need to turn those half-truths into complete lies."

My mouth fell open. Triskén smirked. "All right. Well, I would love to keep my word, but fighting you is just too fun. Now, I'll let Khyonessa recover because you, Khioneus, lack bellicosity and I want an opponent worth fighting."

Nessa stirred and got up. "What happened?"

Her eyes landed on Triskén and flashed with realization.

"Nessa, are you okay? I'm really sorry!" I said.

"I'm fine, but there's a bigger problem, right here!" Nessa gestured toward Triskén. She did not seem fine— her nose was bleeding, and her skin was pale.

"Um, Nessa," I said. "I kind of told Triskén the prophecy . . . "

Nessa turned to me. "Are you crazy? You should have teleported away!"

"And leave Max?" Nessa sighed. She knew I was right.

Telepathically, I said, *I only told Triskén about the* life of the loved one, key to the dark *part. I'm hoping Triskén will be overconfident that its plan will work. Anyway, Triskén knew I was a prophet already.*

Nessa frowned. *We have a lot to discuss with Korukan.*

"Hello! Dangerous entity standing right here, about to kill you," said Triskén. Wolves made of dark smoke appeared around her and charged.

CHAPTER 10

Nessa's Dark Magic

I JUMPED BACK IN TERROR. NESSA immediately created a shield. The wolves bounced off of it but struck again.

I thought about our situation. What was Triskén's weakness? How could we defeat it? Well . . . Nessa could copy magic she's seen before, couldn't she? She had said so herself.

Truly, the only magic that can harm me is my own. That was what Triskén had said.

Nessa, can you copy Triskén's magic?

I don't know. I suppose it's possible. Nessa's telepathic voice had an edge to it, maybe fear. *Should I try?*

Yeah! I said. *Triskén said that its own attacks are the only thing that can harm it. So let's use its magic against it.*

What if something happens to me? Dark magic is unstable.

I hadn't realized that. Never mind then. We can find another way, I said. *Don't do anything you shouldn't do.*

No. I'll try this. It's gonna work. It's gonna *work.* Nessa repeated it like a mantra. She created a whip made of light that slashed through the smoke wolves. She was panting and I knew she was tired.

The Triskén woman transformed into a giant spider and hissed loudly at me, her mandibles clacking. Nessa and I screamed.

"Your screams are damaging my auditory sensors!" said Triskén. "Silence yourselves, or I shall silence you both!" It raised its hand and said, "**Cäthhäx**."

The word had a guttural sound, unlike anything I'd heard in Phantasian. A sphere of darkness appeared in its hand, and Triskén threw it at me. I jumped out of the way, stumbling into Nessa. The sphere sailed off the edge of the tower and sailed into the clouds. Triskén made another dark sphere that flew at Nessa. We both jumped out of the way. The sphere struck the battlements—stone shattered, shards of rock flying in every direction. A gaping hole was left in the crenellation.

I went pale. If that had hit us . . . we would have been blown to gory bits.

That was the curse Nessa could use against Triskén. I looked at Nessa. Her eyes lit up. She winked and said, "**Cäthhäx**."

I don't know how, but she pronounced it correctly, and a black sphere appeared above her hand. She gazed at it in wonder then focused on Triskén. She tossed the black sphere at it. Triskén danced to the side with a silly pirouette.

I frowned. Triskén was too fast! I needed to help Nessa. Maybe I could cast a couple of shield enchantments to hold Triskén in place.

I turned to Nessa. "Can you use the curse again?"

A look of fear came over Nessa's face. "What's wrong?" I asked.

"Nothing." She swallowed. "I'll do it."

"What is it? Did casting the curse do something to you?"

Nessa shook her head, but she seemed hesitant. I pursed my lips.

She cast the curse again. As she threw the ball, I created three invisible shields surrounding Triskén. The black sphere crashed into the creature, and dark smoke splashed all over the **Shielt** enchantments. Suddenly, my eyes and joints burned. I gasped, squeezing my eyes shut until tears took some of the pain away. I instinctively knew the dark smoke hitting the shield enchantments had caused this. I wondered if Nessa was feeling the same.

I opened my eyes. Nessa seemed perfectly fine (albeit pale and her nose still bleeding from before). A formless cloud flashed, flickering with red lights, where Triskén had once been. The curse had hit! But was Nessa really okay or was she just really good at hiding pain?

A voice boomed from the cloud. "You cannot defeat me. **Cäthhäx** shatters *objects*, not *darkness*." Even so, the cloud didn't resolidify into Triskén's body.

"If you can't shatter darkness, what can you do to it?" I said. "You're not even *actual* darkness, Triskén. You're made of *matter*. Darkness is the absence of *photons*, which are *energy*. You're more like a cloud of smoke."

Triskén seemed to ignore that. It said, "**Wespa**."

A beam of darkness shot out of Triskén's mass. Again, we dodged, and the beam hit the edge of the tower. Stones disappeared—poofed into smoke.

Nessa frowned. *Triskén knows I can copy curses, so it's probably a bad idea to copy that one,* she said telepathically. *Or is it using reverse psychology?*

Suddenly, Nessa's eyes lit up.

Triskén cast the curse again. We jumped out of the way just in time.

Nessa said, **"Conjura Mireflecto."**

A mirror appeared in her hand. The next curse Triskén cast slammed into the mirror full force, pushing Nessa backward a little. The magic clung to the glass of the mirror like a rippling film.

"Go ahead, Triskén. Attack me again."

The cloud that was Triskén shrank back.

"Mirrors . . . " came its voice, hostile and growling.

Nessa put her hands on the mirror and said, **"Tolen Tum."**

The dark magic swirled off of the glass and became a cloud in her hands. "I have some of your magic now, and I can get rid of it. **Portuam Confinso Mireflecto**."

The mirror shimmered gold. The dark magic in Nessa's hands flowed into the reflection as if it were another world (which it probably was). Nessa said another spell and the mirror stopped shimmering. Then it vanished.

"You have only weakened me temporarily," said Triskén. "You can't rid the world of all my magic. I am a powerful non-mortal entity that has not been defeated in a half century, with magic as powerful as the angels and as vast as the ocean! My magic is as limitless as human belief. Not even you, Nessa, can defeat me like any material entity. I am not alive."

"Hey, you're right, you *are* nonliving."

I gasped. "Phorthel . . . whatever that was—the light energy thing that only harms nonliving things!"

Nessa smirked. "Phorthelsinphos. And, lucky me, my NOTT amulet allows me to summon weapons from the Hall Ofensia."

The phorthelsinphos gun with a cyan tank on it appeared in her hand. She shot it at Triskén, and part of Triskén's mass flashed with sparks. She shot again and again, and Triskén's mass began disappearing in flashes.

Nessa smirked. "I was a little worried. I wasn't sure if it would work, but you're not made solely of magic, are you? There's some nonmagical, nonliving matter in you, and this gun will vaporize it."

A tendril of darkness reached out toward the gun. Nessa shot the tentacle. It vanished, but more tentacles appeared. Nessa blasted them as well, but there were too many. She muttered a spell, and her gun disappeared.

Triskén gave a mocking laugh.

"Making your fancy gun disappear and reappear is going to take a lot of power. I'll just keep trying to take it from you, until you're too tired to use it."

What do we do? I sent to Nessa.

Nessa looked at me. *We can still use mirrors,* she sent. *We've almost taken enough of its magic to prevent Triskén from using it. Then Triskén's gonna tell me where Max is.*

"**Conjura Quanu hor Demok Mireflecto**!" Several mirrors appeared around her and moved toward Triskén. I tried the same spell while picturing a mirror. It worked! I conjured several mirrors and moved them to Triskén as well. Bits of Triskén flowed toward the mirrors, clinging to them in rippling films.

"I see what you're doing. Clever. You're only trying to sap enough of my magic to prevent me from using it." Triskén's voice was distorted. "For your intelligence I'll give you a reward. Your friend Max is in your very own kingdom, in Neurazia itself."

"What?" Nessa's concentration broke, and the mirrors disappeared. I found that my own mirrors had vanished as well.

Triskén suddenly flared red. The dark mass imploded into nothing, and a shockwave knocked us backward. We caught ourselves just before falling through the hole in the tower's crenellation.

Nessa got up, panting for breath. Both of us were really tired from all of our magic use. "Triskén's disappeared," she said. "That's not good. And it said that Max is in Neurazia! How is that possible?"

Three spheres of energy appeared where Triskén had been, glowing and flaring with yellow electricity. They formed into humanoid shapes, and one of them roared.

Nessa muttered, "It left us a present. Lightning elementals."

One of the elementals shot a bolt of electricity at me. I dodged to the side.

Then I remembered something Metara taught me—the lightning-eating spell. I doubted it would be much use against these powerful elementals, but it was worth a try.

"**Fulminum Diem**!" I said. And just like that, the lightning elementals looked like gingerbread men to my greedy eyes. I leaped at one, using a hoverboard spell to levitate myself from the temple stone. I bit into its shoulder and began to chew. The elemental brought up its horrendous, egg-yolk-colored arms to hit me, but I began eating its arm.

Slowly but surely, it disappeared into my belly. Nessa's eyes sparkled as she realized what I had done, and she dashed up to the next monster and began eating it as well. Either Triskén had been quite dumb to leave *lightning* elementals behind to deal with wizards that could *eat* lightning, or it was playing with us.

Unfortunately, we didn't seem to be hurting them. The monsters regenerated every body part that we ate. We had to stop eating, but I felt strong, full, and very, very magical. "So . . . we didn't hurt them, but at least it made us more powerful," I said.

Nessa sighed. "Humanoid lightning elementals are pretty strong. They're up in the highest tier of lightning elementals."

She closed her eyes, pointed at the elementals, and said, "**Offensia Froscarium.**" Suddenly, the temperature dropped and it began to snow. The snow swirled around the lightning elementals, icicles forming in the tiny blizzard, until Nessa put her hands on her knees, panting.

The snow dispersed. The lightning elementals still stood there—smaller now, and less bright, but still there.

"They withstood a full-scale Setempan blizzard spell! May the gods damn those lightning elementals to an eternity in Tartarös!" cursed Nessa. "Wait! I can teleport the elementals away! **Transporta Zusital Glicer.**"

Huge, stalagmite-type icicles grew around the elementals, encasing them. Suddenly, the ice shattered, leaving behind only ice shards and wisps of blue steam.

Nessa smirked with satisfaction. "There. I sent them to the beach. Wet sand conducts electricity."

"Why didn't you just teleport us somewhere else instead?" I asked.

"We still have to purify the temple, remember?"

She pulled a vial of water out of thin air, then uncapped it and threw the contents in the air while saying a spell. A lot more water than I would have thought spouted from the vial. Nessa raised her hand, and the water rose into the clouds and began to glow. As the stream diminished, a crack of thunder sounded overhead, and glowing clouds spread out from where the stream had been. A warm rain poured, and where the raindrops hit, the temple stone became lighter, the plants greener, and the evil aura around the temple dissipated.

A form materialized in front of me. I stumbled back in surprise. It was Azana, the ghost girl. Her blue glow seemed brighter than before. "Thank you," she said in her echoing voice. "I'm free now."

"You're welcome," I said.

Azana's body glowed even brighter, and a figure appeared behind her. It had the shape of a young man with large wings, but its face was too bright to make out any features. It held one brilliantly shining hand out to Azana. As she took it, the air flashed, and a blue portal appeared, swirling like the ocean. The two figures floated into the portal and disappeared in a flash.

As they vanished, white orbs appeared in the air. The orbs burst in shards of what appeared to be ice. I picked one shard up and squinted at it, my eyes still hurting from that flash and the figure's brilliance. It hummed, and I smelled the odor of fish and brine, like the one that permeated the piers in San Francisco. I coughed and realized it was the odor of dark magic I had smelled when we first came to the temple.

The shard leaped out of my hand. All the shards floated toward each other. They joined with a flash and became a translucent white key.

"Nessa!" I said. "The key—it was trapped in Azana's ghostly enchantments!" I turned back to Nessa. She was lying on the ground, her eyes closed.

Horror-struck, I ran to her and shook her. Her eyes opened, unfocused. She mumbled, "I'm fine. Stop shaking me."

"Can you get up?"

"No," she said. "I want to sleep."

I looked around in a panic. How was I going to get her back home? I tried picking her up and discovered she was pretty light—almost dangerously so. She groaned as I moved her.

"Nessa, what's the teleport spell?"

Her faint voice floated to my ears. "My teleporter's in the bag on my belt. The passcode is Imi-Nixa."

I reached into the bag—it was a lot bigger on the inside than on the outside—and groped for the teleporter. Finally, I pulled it out and fiddled with it, finding Neurazia's gate on the map and pressing the button.

We appeared in front of the gate, and I said the password. I used the teleporter again to get to the Hall Remenda. Thankfully, Metara was there. She looked up in shock as I gently set Nessa down in front of her. Man, Nessa *was* light, but my arms were sore from carrying her.

Metara went to work right away with healing spells. "Nessa has some strange mutation of malmagiopathosis," she said. "I can ionize her blood to try and extract some—"

"Okay, just do it," I said.

A small black cat, who I assumed was her pet, curled up next to Nessa. Tired, I used the door portal to go to the throne room and tell Father what happened.

He immediately followed me to Hall Remenda, relaxing when he saw Metara caring for Nessa.

Suddenly, Nessa started screaming strange things over and over. "*JODOVÑA! JODOVÑA! VE VÉNEJODOVÑA!*"

Tears slid down her face, and then she cried out my name. "*KHIONEUS-HI JA VÉNEHÏKHAR! Gonda ops ve ja gopu?*"

"What is she *saying*? What language is this?"

"I don't know," Father said. "I'll cast a translation spell. **Textransferrum Sumar Levinga.**"

It didn't work, the screaming still unintelligible to us. Finally, Nessa fell into a deep sleep. Father, Metara, and I stayed with her for the rest of the night. None of us slept. Metara said that none of her cures were working. She could cast most healing spells without potions, but even she couldn't help Nessa.

She said all we could do was wait. I was scared. Even in her current state, Nessa kept muttering—prayers, my name, those weird words she said before, strangled screams, and other things. It was unnerving, like she was possessed or something.

Nessa woke up, lucid, at three in the morning. I hugged her hard. She laughed and told me that a silly fever couldn't take her out that easily, but I knew it hadn't just been a fever.

Even so, she seemed perfectly fine and wanted to go to the NOTT headquarters right away.

Korukan asked for the whole story, despite Nessa's protests that she was fine. I was nervous retelling how I had told Triskén part of the prophecy, but Korukan simply sighed and said, "Nessa's life is worth more than the prophecy. You did well. Besides, you didn't tell Triskén all of it."

I showed Korukan the key, much to both his and Nessa's surprise. "Keep it with you," he said. "You two are quite special. Nessa can copy any spell or enchantment that exists, and you . . . Not only are you a prophet, but when the unicorn tried to kill you, you *broke* its curse. One can make magic, the other breaks it. I'm willing to bet you two will have a large part to play in Elkloria's future. So keep the key, but . . . maybe we should put it in a magnesium-weave bag. It's emitting a lot of dark magic. Magnesium will contain its aura." Korukan wrinkled his nose and left to get a bag from the back room.

I looked at the key. The blue gem inlaid in it felt like an eye staring up at me.

CHAPTER 11

Max

WE WALKED INTO THE HALLWAY OUTSIDE the NOTT
chamber. I turned to Nessa.

"Nessa, do you want to . . . "

Nessa rolled her eyes. "What do you want, Khi?"

"You don't have to snap at me," I said, hurt. "I was just
going to ask if you wanted to take a walk."

"I'm sorry. I just feel cranky. Maybe I'm not as well as I
thought." She sighed. "And I miss Max."

I looked at my feet and nodded. "I miss him, too. We
need to clear our heads—you getting sick combined with
Max being sacrificed and the demon portal opening in
four days is a lot of stress on us."

"Ha. I don't know about you, but I already had that
much stress in my life. Anyway, where are we going?"

"Maybe a restaurant? But I don't know what's good here."

She thought about it. "How about Consio hor Drakonai Acule? It's got great food."

I nodded. Nessa produced an eye-disguise amulet seemingly from thin air (where did she keep all those amulets, anyway?) and handed it to me.

So, we set off on our journey to the restaurant, with many complaints from Nessa about using the "broken-down, junky old tube" to travel between layers. I told her she couldn't use the teleporter like she always did because it might disorient her, and she was in fragile condition. That annoyed her a lot.

As we walked, bugs buzzed around my face. I waved my hand to shoo the nasty critters away, but realized they weren't bugs. They were pixies—little girls and boys with elfin ears and wings fluttering around me, chattering about everything. They babbled about cool, new pixie gadgets or their awesome toys or a popular new human singer, Kya (apparently, her first song had been an instant hit), or who liked whom or whatever. Some asked me what hairstyle or dress I liked best, magically changing their appearance in front of me until I picked one. Some asked me to be a tiebreaker in their arguments about sports or shoe brands. Some even asked me for relationship advice. As if I knew any-thing about that!

"Who are you talking to?" asked Nessa.

"The pixies," I said, gesturing to the cloud of little humanoids fluttering around me.

She gave me a strange look. "Khi . . . pixies can't speak Common Tongue."

"Okay. If you say so."

Nessa shrugged, seeming uninterested in talking.

⚜ ⚜ ⚜

THE RESTAURANT WAS A CUTE BUILDING with warm windows and a sign on the roof that said Consio hor Drakonai Acule.

At our table, a tall server came up to take our orders. I ordered a burger (it's strange but nice that Elkloria has foods that are like the ones back home), and Nessa ordered a salad. We both ordered lemonade. As the server took our orders, I noticed Nessa winking at him and subtly flirting. The server noticed too, because he was considerably more red-faced when he left our table.

"I wonder whether the fact you're flirting with servers means that you're in perfect health," I sighed.

"Why did you order such a small salad?" I asked. "Shouldn't you order more?"

Nessa leaned in nervously and said, "I need to lose some weight, so I'm going on a diet."

Diet? With a body that thin? She didn't need to be any thinner!

A different server brought us our food. She had black makeup and piercings, a curtain of spiky hair, and a cross expression on her face—unnerving, but I decided that I

THE DOOR TO INFERNA

shouldn't judge her based on her looks. She probably was a kind, sweet person.

After the server left, Nessa took a bite of salad. Suddenly, her eyes became unfocused, and she fell face-first onto her plate.

"Nessa?" I yelped, shaking her. She didn't move. I reached for her neck to feel her pulse. Thank goodness, she was alive.

I looked around to see if anyone could help us, but we were in a very secluded part of the restaurant (Nessa had decided the normal restaurant area wasn't good enough for her). That's when the waitress materialized next to Nessa, holding a knife to Nessa's throat.

"Maledictum Soliven," I said, but the spell didn't do anything. There was no echo to my voice. The words were . . . just words. Nessa said that a spell was like a powerful force locked behind a door, and the words were the key that released it. But the door wasn't there, and I was just turning the key in empty air. My magic felt all wrong, like someone was inflating it or something. It felt trapped inside me, unable to get out of my body.

Suddenly we were in a different place. Part of the restaurant booth had come with us, sheared clean away, as if someone had cut out a sphere of the universe with us in it and moved it here. Two tall figures in hooded cloaks with long, flared sleeves stood near us. We floated in the air, the vines glowing and pulsing around us.

The taller of the two figures said, "Our experiment might go very well. These two seem to hold much magic power."

I opened my mouth to say something when the creepy waitress jabbed my rear with something. (Ow! Why?! Couldn't she just have used magic on me instead?) I slipped away into incomprehensible oblivion.

⚜ ⚜ ⚜

I CAME TO FEELING VERY COLD. I was still suspended above the ground by those dark green vines, which didn't seem to be attached to anything, trailing off into thin air. I was trapped inside a glass cage.

Something inside me vibrated, like I was getting a text message in my heart. A glow appeared on my chest, barely visible through my robe. I could feel it in my skin, cold like metal.

Suddenly, the glass walls around me shattered, the vines ripped free (from whatever invisible thing they were attached to), and I fell to the ground surrounded by shards of glass. That was strange—no spell or anything. Was it because I was the prophetic vessel of a deity? Was the god of fate helping me out? No . . . Nessa said prophets had supernatural knowledge, not powers.

I picked my way across the broken glass. My magic still felt blocked, and the glow on my chest was gone. Several glass containers like the one I had been trapped in stood around me in a dark space that I couldn't see the ends of. Nessa was in the container next to mine, unconscious and suspended by vines.

I ran to her and examined the container to see if there was any way to get her out. I found a red panel on the back with a single button, a hole underneath it, and a red light above it. The button was inscribed with odd symbols:

My finger hovered over the button as I debated. Should I press it? Would it hurt Nessa or get her out? "Mr. Fate God, sir, it would be great if you could help me out here, maybe with some, you know, prophetic advice . . . or actually, you're not going to help me, because you only give me prophecies when I don't need them, like before I knew I was a prophet." I wondered if the fate god would ever give me prophecies again.

I circled the cage again, looking for any other way to open it. I tried hitting it with my fist, but that just hurt my hand. I didn't even crack the glass (though I think it would have hurt my hand even worse if I had). I wrapped one of the vines around my fist and tried again. Still nothing. I even tried sticking the vine into the hole under the button. I desperately wished Nessa could help me, but she was out cold.

I investigated the rest of the room. It was lit dimly by small, glowing orbs high up near the ceiling. The room was empty except for the cages and a door with a panel on it. The panel showed a very large keypad with strange symbols in the same language as the button—probably a password box. So, I couldn't leave the room anyway without a password.

I suddenly had an idea. I looked for the symbols from the button on Nessa's cage. There were so many symbols that searching for each took a while, which made me question the keypad's efficiency for typing passwords.

The symbols didn't work. Obviously.

I decided my only choices were to press the button or leave Nessa and hope for a way to free her somewhere else. The second choice seemed dangerous. So did the first, but it seemed safer than leaving her.

I went back to Nessa's cage and pressed the button.

A vine snaked down from above. I looked up in shock and saw an enormous pipe in the ceiling, too high to reach.

The vine inserted itself into the hole under the button and glowed with a rhythmic pulse. Immediately, the vines around Nessa pulsed as well, and the panel light turned green. Black lines like circuitry worked their way across her skin. I watched in horror. Nessa was going to die because of me—just like Max!

No. Lamenting the past wouldn't fix anything. I had to find a way to help her. I smacked the button again, but nothing happened. Nessa's eyes snapped open, pure red and glowing. Cracks snaked across the glass walls. I dashed away from it just as it exploded. Nessa fell to the ground, and I ran over to her. The light orbs suddenly went out with a shower of blue sparks, and a dim red light turned on above us. What had just happened?

I shook her awake. "Nessa?"

She looked around in a daze. Her eyes rested on me. "Where are we? What happened?"

Then her eyes widened. "Wait! We were eating at Consio hor Drakonai Acule and then . . . then . . . "

I helped her out. "That server with the dark makeup, remember her? She teleported us here, and there were these creepy people in hoods, and I was in this cage, and you were in another cage, and I tried getting you out a bunch of ways. The only one that worked was pressing that button."

I pointed to the panel, which was now lying on the ground. She looked at it and scowled.

"That button says 'injection!' Why would you press random buttons without knowing the consequences? Are you crazy?"

"It was the only choice I had! And what language is that, anyway?"

Nessa raised an eyebrow. "Looks like Common Tongue to me."

"I can't read it though. All I see are strange symbols."

"How did an 'injection' get me out of that cage, anyway?" muttered Nessa. "How did you get out?"

"My answer to both those questions is I don't know. Are you okay?"

Nessa shrugged. "I'm fine."

"You sure?" I asked.

"Don't worry about it," she said. "We need to figure out where we are and how to get out . . . "

"Without magic," I said.

She looked around her for the first time. "Oh, by the damnedest pits of Inferna! Enkyron!"

"Enkyron?"

"Iron imbued with a special potion that makes magic unusable. Anyway, how do we get out of this place?"

"Well," I said, "there's a keypad by the door over there. Can you figure it out?"

Nessa walked over to it. "This panel seems to be turned off." She tapped it, and it sparked. "Whoa!"

Text appeared on the screen: "POWER LOW. SHUTTING DOWN."

"You know," I said, "before I pressed the injection button, the room was pretty well lit. Once I pressed it, the lights turned off and that red light came on."

"So we're trapped here." Nessa angrily whacked the panel, and suddenly the door opened. "Oh . . . wow! What horrible craftsmanship."

We walked into a second, smaller room with two additional doors. Both had signs with strange symbols on it.

132

Nessa could read these, too. "One says 'exit.' The other says . . . Portal Sacrifice?"

I gasped. "Remember what Triskén said about Max?"

Nessa's eyes widened. "It said he was in Neurazia! I thought it was trying to break my concentration for that spell. I didn't think it was telling the truth . . . could that mean Max is here?"

For the first time since Max was kidnapped, I felt hope. "Let's go check that Portal Sacrifice room!"

I ran my hands over the door, feeling for some kind of opening mechanism. I pushed on it, but it didn't budge. Nessa pushed with me, and it moved! With our combined strength, the door opened unexpectedly easily. Inside was a room walled with dark stone. A single light shone in the center, and in the back was a large door, barely visible. The door had a keyhole.

As if with a mind of their own, my fingers reached into my pocket and pulled out the magnesium-weave bag. The creepy waitress must not have found it or else thought nothing of it because the magnesium blocked the key's aura. I walked to the keyhole.

"Khi," said Nessa. "Is this smart?"

I shrugged. "Who knows? All I know is I have a key and Max could be imprisoned here."

"But the key you're holding is the key to the Wildlandes," said Nessa. "According to the prophecy. I highly doubt it will be the right key."

"It can't hurt, can it?"

"Yes, it can definitely hurt," said Nessa nervously. "What if you trigger an alarm?"

But all I could think about was that Max could be in here. Nessa sighed and followed me, an apprehensive look on her face. I put the key in the keyhole.

It clicked! I opened the door to reveal a small room. A door with a keyhole the same shape as the first one waited on the opposite wall. In the center of the room was a bed. Max lay on it.

Max opened his eyes as I came near. He got up slowly and blinked at me.

"Wow. This is probably the best dream I've had since I was captured," he said.

"Max!" I ran to him and hugged him. "It's me, Khi!"

He rolled his eyes. "Yes, dream-Khi, I know who you are. And I'm guessing that now that I know this is a dream, I'm going to wake up. I just wish you would be here when I woke up."

"What do you mean? I'm not a dream! I'm really here!"

Max frowned. "Huh. I'm not waking up." He grinned. "I might as well enjoy my dream." Then he leaned forward and kissed me on the lips.

I jumped back in shock. "MAX! What the heck?" The sweet reunion had just become strange. I was still happy, but now I was also very confused.

Max looked terrified. He noticed Nessa behind me and said a word I won't repeat.

"You . . . you came! This isn't a dream!"

"Yeah, we came," I said. "But why did you . . . you know . . . ?"

Max reddened. "Um . . . "

Nessa interrupted, sounding panicked. "Important stuff happening!"

I turned. Several people stood in the doorway wearing hooded cloaks with the words "Ex Morte" on them beneath skulls with snakes coming out of their eyes. One of them turned to one of the others and spoke, an angry male voice from the dark recesses of the hood.

"Those are the special subjects she requested. What are they doing here?"

Who was she? Triskén?

The one who spoke strode slowly toward us, raising his hands.

I turned to Nessa. "What can we do? We've got no magic!"

Then I remembered the door at the back of Max's cell. I ran over to it, put the key in the lock, and turned. The three of us ran out into blinding sunlight.

The hooded people ran after us when a rumble shook the room behind us. Dark shapes dropped from the ceiling. Before I could make out what they were, the door we came through flickered and vanished. We were standing in a forest of spindly black trees with orange leaves shaped like tiny flames. The ground had a yellow tinge, and the sky above looked like a raging inferno. An enormous volcano loomed in the distance, smoke pouring from its top like it was about to erupt. It was sweltering hot—dark, wet patches covered my robe, and we'd only been there for five minutes.

"What in Psymus's power?" said Nessa. "I've seen pictures of this place. We're in the Wildlandes!"

CHAPTER 12

Wildlandes

"THAT'S NOT POSSIBLE," SAID MAX, "THE Wildlandes are really far—across the entire ocean. The rules of magic are pretty clear about saltwater messing up spatial magic. It's not possible to teleport across the ocean!"

Nessa said, "Apparently, Triskén can break the rules of spatial magic."

I began hyperventilating, forgetting all about Max's kiss. "Oh my god. We're in the land of demons! We're an entire ocean away from Neurazia, and the portal we came through is gone!"

"Khi!" said Nessa. "KHI!"

"What?"

"Look, Max and I are both experienced in magic. We'll figure out how to get home, okay? Don't worry. Everything will be alright. We can't teleport, but we can use magic to contact our parents and the NOTT."

Max nodded.

I closed my eyes, taking a deep breath to calm myself down. Then I remembered. "Max . . . why did you do that?" Max looked nervous. "Do what?"

"You know," I said quietly.

"Hey, you know what?" Nessa said a little too loudly. "I'm going to look for a nice clearing to set up a campsite in." She walked away, disappearing between two trees.

Max looked down. "Khi, I . . . I thought I was dreaming."

"Why did you kiss me, though?" I asked.

Max squeezed his eyes shut. A tear slid out of his eye. "I can't believe this is happening—not like this."

My heart twinged. "I'm sorry, Max. I didn't mean to . . . call you out or . . . "

Max sniffled. "I just . . . my God, Khi, I like you. More than you like me. More than a friend. More than I should, because you consider me a brother. I didn't want you to find out this way. I didn't want you to ever find out. I hoped it would just fade away, because I didn't want to compromise our friendship."

I swallowed. "How long have you . . . ?"

Max laughed humorlessly. "Since I figured out that giddy feeling I had around you meant 'L-O-V-E.'" His fingers sketched air quotes. "I guess it was a crush, but it grew over the years. Guys at school talked about girls and called gay guys horrible names. I was scared—terrified

THE DOOR TO INFERNA

that I was a 'homo.' It took time, and love from my parents, whom I told, for me to finally accept myself. Still . . . I was afraid to tell you. I didn't know how you felt. I knew you hated it when people called gay guys bad names, and you always told them to stop, but I wasn't sure what that meant. Was it a front? Were you gay? I was afraid of what you would think of me, but I think I was more afraid of what would happen if you didn't like me back—or if you did like me back."

"Look . . . Max." Tears pooled at the corners of my own eyes. "I . . . I don't like you back. I don't . . . feel that way. I just . . . I don't know. I'm sorry."

Max sniffled. Then his tears spilled over, and he was full-on crying. Between sobs he gasped, "I . . . I know. I've b . . . been t . . . trying to prepare myself, b-but I . . . n-now that I'm f . . . faced with the t-t-truth, it's a lot harder to d-deal with than I thought."

A tear fell from my eye as well. I put my arms around him. He tensed and then melted into my embrace. "Look, Max," I said quietly. "I won't pretend to under- stand what you're feeling, but I'm here for you. I can't be here for you as a boyfriend, but I can be your best friend."

Max hugged me back. I pulled away and looked him in the eyes. "Seriously, though, I'll be your friend no matter what. Even if you have feelings for me and can't stand to be around me because it's too painful. I'll wait for you."

Max averted his eyes from mine. We sat like that for a few moments, me looking at Max and him staring at the ground.

"We should go check out Nessa's campsite," Max said. The abrupt change of topic surprised me a little, and we both got up.

Max and I followed in the direction Nessa had gone. We found Nessa drawing symbols on the ground around a simple tent made from canvas and sticks. The oddness of what she was doing stopped me for a second.

She looked up and waited, watching us appraisingly. "So . . . what happened?"

"I told Khi I had feelings for him, and he said he didn't have feelings for me," sighed Max. "What are you doing?"

"I drew a runic protection structure to protect our tent from demons. Now, maybe we can contact the NOTT, though I don't know if this communication amulet will work over the ocean."

Nessa muttered a spell, and her eyes glazed over. A device appeared in her hand. She pressed some buttons then looked up, annoyed.

"Neither the amulet's nor the teleporter's communication system work," she said.

"Try using shared magical spaces to communicate," asked Max.

Nessa closed her eyes for a second, muttering spells, then shook her head.

"Shoot," said Max. "What about cyberspatial communication?"

Nessa shook her head. "Tried it."

I was getting scared. If magic didn't work over the ocean, we could be trapped in the most dangerous place on the planet forever. "Are there any flight spells either of you can use from your everything-magic to at least see which way the ocean is?"

Nessa nodded. "Yeah." Her body began to glow and distort. Suddenly, she was a dragon—a beautiful, iridescent black dragon with a shimmering violet mane and eyes that shone gold.

She flew into the sky, wheeled around for a minute, and then flew back down.

"I can't see the ocean from here," she said. "But that volcano in the distance can act as a beacon. If we ever get separated, we should meet there."

Awe overcame my fear. "Wow, Nessa, that was amazing! How did you do that?"

Nessa shrugged. "I'm Polymorphik. I can change forms. Polymorphizm is magigenetic but very rare."

I felt a little put out. "Oh. I can't do that, can I?"

Nessa shrugged. "You might be able to. Let's check. Use the Telekinesia spell. It moves objects."

I didn't see how moving objects was related to Polymorphizm, but I shrugged and cast the spell (which was surprisingly easy to cast) on a small rock nearby.

"Use it like an extension of your arm," said Nessa. "Move your arm, and your invisible, telekinetic arm will move as well."

I moved my arm up, and the pebble moved up. The pebble seemed to be held up by a sort of translucent bowl that looked like it was made of energy. The bowl was half blue and half white, a straight line between the two colors.

"That bowl thing is the aural energy that acts as your telekinetic hand," said Max.

"Your aura has two colors!"

Nessa said, "Khi must be Bimorphik! The two colors must be his forms! A human form and one other form!"

I was so excited I jumped up and down like a kid. "Seriously? That's so cool! What other form do I have?"

Nessa shrugged. "I don't know."

"How do I change?" I asked.

"Well," said Nessa. "You should use a simple spell. It's very hard to change without it the first time, but after that you can simply imagine the form to change. The Bimorphizm spell is Sumar Transformoa."

"Okay," I said. "Suma—"

"Wait!" said Max. "Your clothes. They'll rip apart if you change form."

My cheeks colored. "Please don't tell me I have to take them off."

"There's a spell that primes the clothes you're wearing to vanish and reappear whenever you change form or teleport," said Max. "The magical wardrobe spell."

Max taught me the spell, and I used it on my current clothes. Then I said, "**Sumar Transformoa**."

I found myself floating in a starry space. A glowing white doorway floated in front of me. I could feel my body floating and standing in the sweltering heat of the Wildlandes at the same time.

I wasn't sure what to do, so I focused on the white doorway. I floated through it into bright sunlight.

I was back in the Wildlandes, but it wasn't as hot anymore, and I was a lot taller. My senses had heightened—I could see farther, see more colors, and hear movements several hundred feet away. I could smell something like strawberry yogurt from Nessa and cinnamon from Max. Both smells were permeated with a nasty pungency that I associated with sweat. I memorized the smells and realized I was doing what dogs did—identifying via smells.

I looked at my body. It was huge and covered in white, pearlescent scales. My legs were strong, sporting long, icy blue claws.

I felt a sort of presence between my shoulder blades— two actually. I mentally reached out and flexed muscles I didn't have before.

I leapt off the ground for a second, propelled by . . . my wings. They were large and bat-like, catching the light and refracting it like a crystal.

"Whoa!" I said, except my draconic mouth never moved. The sound just kind of radiated out from me. "I can fly!"

I flapped my wings experimentally a few more times and fluttered up, then I tumbled through the air and crashed into a bunch of trees. The trees broke, but I was unhurt.

"Khi!" yelped Nessa. "Don't be so loud! You don't know what you might alert in the Wildlandes."

"Sorry," I whispered.

I imagined my body becoming human and turned back into myself. My clothes were intact, thankfully.

Nessa smiled. "You've got the same creature as me for your other form. That's kinda cool."

I suddenly felt a sharp pain in the middle of my chest and another on the upper half of my right hamstring. I yelped.

"Are you okay?" said Max, concerned.

Nessa said, "Did you feel sharp pains just now?"

I nodded, a little surprised. Nessa said, "That was the creation of your Bimorphik marks. They look like birthmarks in the shapes of your forms—one will be human and the other dragon. These birthmarks are your form connections. If someone were to cast a disconnecting spell on one of them, you would lose that form and be trapped in the other."

I couldn't resist. I discreetly pulled open the top buttons of my robe and peeked at the perfectly rendered shape of a humanoid on my chest. I didn't attempt the weird angles I would need to see the other.

After the excitement of my Polymorphizm, we realized

all of us were disgusting, so Nessa created a bathtub made of magic along with a small bar of soap. Max conjured new clothes for me and taught me how to conjure them myself. We bathed one at a time.

One need taken care of, we realized we had no food. Max set about conjuring ingredients, while Nessa muttered something about communication networks and sat down on a little chair she conjured a short distance away. A glowing panel floated in the air in front of her. Lines of text scrolled across the panel, and Nessa typed on a holographic keyboard.

Unfortunately, I had nothing to do. Max had given me some holy water (which was not actual water—more like lamp oil infused with holy magic) and a small amulet that would create a dome shield in case of demons. I decided to explore the forest around the campsite, knowing that if, by some chance, I met a demon while walking around, I'd be able to protect myself.

I noticed a strange rosebush—it would have been beautiful if the roses were not pitch black. The smell was not as bad as dark Aethelum, but it was close.

I used the telekinetic spell to pick a rose from a distance. Suddenly, I felt a sharp burning pain like the one I had felt when Nessa's dark spell hit my shield spell in the temple. My force-hand vanished, and the rose fell. I decided not to get near it. It seemed to dispel magic, and I had a feeling I would need all my resources in the Wildlandes.

I walked a little further and found my way blocked by a bunch of thorny brambles covered in pink flowers. Once again, I used the telekinetic spell (such a useful spell!) to push aside the brambles so I could step through. My robe snagged on one of the brambles and before I realized it, a piece of my robe tore off and one of the thorns scratched my shoulder.

Suddenly, the brambles closed around me, dark fog swirling between them. I panicked, afraid I had awakened some demonic entity hungry for my blood. I sighed in relief when the fog cleared and the brambles reopened.

I felt uncomfortable, like I didn't want to adventure any further. Deciding to go back toward camp, I turned and walked right into a tree. Where had that come from?

As I picked my way between the trees back to the clearing, I realized all the trees were wrong.

I reached a clearing, but its shape was wrong. More importantly, no one was there.

Maybe I'd gone in the wrong direction. I hadn't ventured far. They had to be close.

"Nessa? Max?" I called.

No one answered.

The brambles . . . They must have teleported me somewhere when they scratched me.

Nessa and Max could be anywhere. I could be anywhere.

I was all alone in the Wildlandes. I didn't have the others to help me.

I took deep breaths to calm myself down. Okay, Khi, put aside your fear and think. How can you find the others?

I looked at the volcano, which was super big—visible even now. Nessa said we should meet there if we ever got separated.

I started walking, then remembered that my dragon form could fly! That would definitely be faster, and the air would probably be refreshingly cool up high.

But flying proved futile. The air above the trees was hot and smoky. I practically choked on it before spiraling to the ground.

When I hit the ground, I transformed back and realized I forgot to cast the magical wardrobe spell on my new clothes—they were lying in shreds around me. I blushed, even though no one was there. I conjured new clothes, this time casting the wardrobe spell in case I needed to transform again.

Resigned, I began walking toward the volcano again. Once again, my way-too-slow memory pinged, and I remembered the speed spell Max and Metara had used when I first came to Elkloria.

"**Rappidum**," I said. Immediately, I shot forward so fast I nearly crashed into a tree. I stopped running and took a deep breath. After I crashed into two more trees, I gave up on the spell.

Something crunched behind me—like a twig or leaves. I wasn't alone.

CHAPTER 13

Witches and Demons

A BEAUTIFUL, BLACK-HAIRED WOMAN GLIDED INTO view. She wore a long black dress and had pale yellow eyes—almost white in their luminescence. She wore a necklace with a green pendant. Her bare feet floated above the ground.

"What are you doing here, child?" she asked in a melodic voice. "You do not have the dark soulless eyes of a warlock or the fiery aura of a demon."

I backed away slowly from this strange apparition. My voice shook. "Who are you?"

"My name is Elesebedä. I am a witch of the Zintera coven. And you?"

"Wait a second, you're a witch? Like eat-children-in-gingerbread-houses, deal-with-the-Christian-Devil witch?"

She laughed. "Your ideas are quite silly. No self-respecting witch would eat a child! Perhaps you are thinking of warlocks. They are like witches, but evil."

"So . . . are you evil? Or are these warlocks evil?" I pulled the holy water out of my pocket carefully, keeping it behind my back.

"No, child, witches serve the light, though we do use dark magic. Warlocks serve the darkness. They are almost always men, and we witches are almost always women. Witches and warlocks are mortal enemies.

"The Wildlandes is our holy land. Warlocks come here on pilgrimages, but they are very dangerous. You must leave soon, or you may find yourself in a titanium cage or a nasty warlock potion."

Well, I was already planning to run.

A sickly-sweet voice came from behind me. "Ah, Lady Elesebedä, head of the Zintera coven. We meet again. What a pleasure."

Elesebedä's eyes narrowed. "Atākhäfe. What are you doing here, you foul being?"

I turned to see a handsome, dark-haired man wearing a thick, symbol-covered robe behind me. His smile looked cruel. His eyes were black as oil.

Elesebedä looked at me. "Child, you cannot stay here. Leave now!"

Atākhäfe said, "A human boy. In the Wildlandes!"

He suddenly lunged for me, but Elesebedä threw some sort of powder at him.

He froze in midair, his black-nailed fingers inches from me. I ran. I ran through the trees, smacking into branches, tripping and falling into puddles that weren't there a second before. Demonic birds with red eyes and horns attacked out of nowhere, until I was too far from the warlock for him to affect me.

I looked back. A flash of white light clashed with a dark smokiness above the treetops where the witch and warlock had been.

When I turned around, I came face to face with a teenage boy with curving horns and glowing eyes. His fingers had claws, a tufted tail swished behind him, wings sprouted from holes in his jacket, and fangs poked from behind his jet-black lips. I was quite sure at this point he was a demon.

He wore a black leather jacket that only went halfway down his torso. He had black cropped jeans and chains around his neck. He wore a black, backward-facing cap (with holes for his horns). The shirt underneath his open jacket, which had a spiky hem and a row of diamond-shaped holes down each side, showed a picture of a skull with a long tongue that had a bunch of glyphs underneath it.

"Whoa! Who're you?" said the demon.

I jumped back, unable to speak. "What did you do with your horns? Are you even a human?" The demon had a confused smile on his face, his head slightly tilted.

I held out my hand and tried to conduit enough magic power to my hands to make them glow. I gave him what I hoped was a threatening look. I probably looked as threatening as a puppy. Hopefully, my glowing hands would help.

"Don't come near me."

The demon's smile turned into a look of shock. "Please don't shoot fireballs at me! I don't mean any harm. I'm Hebïra, from Erebos City. I come in peace?" He sniffed the air. "Hey, something smells good. Is there food nearby?"

His eyes, as well as his nose, turned to me, and I felt afraid.

"Wait a second . . . you're the food that I'm smelling! But you don't smell normal . . . You're like nothing I've ever smelled before. You smell alien."

His eyes widened. "By the sun gods, where the heck am I? And what the heck are you? Are you . . . a goblin? But those . . . don't exist. They're mythical. This is crazy! How do you speak English? Hold still, I wanna take a picture of you."

He reached into his pocket. I was puzzled. He called me a goblin—why? I didn't know much about demons, besides the obvious fact that they invented evil. That could be biased . . . but I didn't want to find out. Did demon society equate humans with some sort of mischievous mythical creatures?

Also, he said the word English. I realized I wasn't understanding the demon like normal. I was understanding his intent. I remembered Lianaka saying the Wildlandes were a dimundial place—a place of two worlds. Maybe that's why I could understand the demon without knowing its language.

Suddenly, Hebïra clutched his head. "Oww! What are you . . . doing . . . to me?"

A glowing liquid oozed over his eyes, until they looked like solid gold. He growled, sending chills down my spine. His voice became primal, animalistic, filled with rage and hunger, as if something was possessing him. "You are a creature of the Aelkiram. You must die! We shall tear you apart and consume your insides!" His teeth elongated into tusks, his claws lengthened, and his body bulked up a bit, making him look feral.

Aelkiram was Phantasian for Fae. I was confused and scared. It was like demonic possession, except Hebïra was already a demon, so . . .

Hebïra snarled and jumped at me, drool dripping from his lips. I jumped away. As he stumbled past me, it was as if some aura of his clung to me. I felt a horrible revulsion, and I felt more afraid than I already was. I backed away, trying to calm my racing heart before I fainted.

Hebïra held out his hand, and a fireball shot out of it. I dodged out of the way. He flew up on dark, bat-like wings and then plunged down at me, claws extended. I created a Shielt Fisicus, and Hebïra crashed into it. He screeched in anger, and I felt that aura of darkness again.

Another fireball hit the shield. He roared. "Ow! We don't like the magic of the Aelkiram! Stop defending yourself and accept death!"

"No chance!"

Hebïra pointed at a branch above my head. It broke and fell toward me, dripping steaming goo as if someone had cut it with acid. I barely got my shield up in time. The weight of the branch on my arms made me cry out in pain. Without the shield, I might have broken my arms. A small blob fell from where the branch broke and bit my arm. I shook my arm wildly, and the blob flew far above Hebïra and over the trees.

Suddenly, Hebïra disappeared. In his place crawled a swarm of spiders. They flowed toward me in a wave, up my body, smothering me. I was paralyzed, too scared to move as they bit me all over. I finally gained my wits (some of them), and started screaming and jumping about, whacking the spiders off me. They were illusions! When I flicked one, it disappeared. The spiders faded away, and I could see Hebïra again. The glowing fluid on his eyes roiled angrily, and I found myself unable to wrench my gaze from his.

My mind became hazy. I found myself pondering the imbalance in the number of leaves on either side of a branch above Hebïra's head.

Hebïra became the only thing I knew or could remember. What was my name? Did I have a family? Where was I? Where did I live? What was I thinking about just now? None of it mattered.

"Walk here," rumbled Hebïra. I sluggishly moved my legs. Hebïra shot a fireball at me, and some instinct made me jump back.

The demon screeched, "Walk to me!"

I began walking back toward Hebïra. As I got closer, a feeling of wrongness overcame me, horror, like the aura from before. I felt a sudden, sharp pain in my pinky. My hypnotism broke! I was confused for a second then jumped back as I realized I was two feet from Hebïra.

I looked down to see the little green blob from before. I instinctively kicked it away.

Then I felt bad as it sailed into a bush. That little green blob had saved me.

I shot an Ofensia spell at Hebïra, hoping to surprise the consciousness behind his luminiferous eyes, but Hebïra evaded quickly. The spell hit a small rock behind him, shattering it into pieces. I shot the sunlight spell. He screamed in pain. I felt bad, because it seemed like Hebïra himself had no bad intent—only the demonic entity inside him.

I wondered if the things Elklorians said about demons were only because of the predatory creatures that forced them to attack humans.

Then I remembered the holy water.

I pulled it out of my pocket. It looked and smelled like water, though Max said it was a bit sweeter and had an explosive reaction with dark magic. The holy water in the vial was pressurized and would shoot out if I uncapped the vial.

I started to unscrew the cap.

But I couldn't. I couldn't kill Hebïra. He was a victim. My enemy was the demonic consciousness in Hebïra's body. I put the holy water away.

I wasn't sure I could kill the demonic consciousness anyway. Killing another sentient being . . . it was a horrible thought.

Running out of options, I turned into a dragon. I felt a lot safer; I was at least much taller and stronger than Hebïra now. My throat tingled. Dragons could breathe fire! Maybe I could trap Hebïra in a ring of fire . . .

I had to try. I opened my mouth. Silver dragonfire flowed out like liquid energy. It swirled in a cylinder, like clouds made of flame.

The cylinder surrounded Hebïra. Translucent rainbow crystals grew everywhere it touched, trapping Hebïra in an iridescent prison.

Wow. Way better than normal fire.

Through the distorted prison, Hebïra's eyes stopped glowing. His body shrunk, his clothing tattered. "Wha . . . what happened?" he said. "Where am I?"

While Hebïra dazedly looked around his prison, I turned back into a human and ran.

Like most magic, the dragonfire would probably wear off eventually.

I was glad to have escaped both a warlock and a demon, but now it was getting dark—the flaming maelstrom in the sky was turning purple. I set up a temporary camp, using the amulet Max had given me to cast a shield.

As I tried to sleep, I saw a dark shape in the distance and heard roaring. Pungent waves of Dark Aethelum flooded my sinuses. I sincerely hoped the dark shape wasn't going to be an enemy in the future, but I supposed that would be too much to hope for. After a few minutes of worrying, my exhaustion took over and I fell asleep.

The next day, I packed up camp and moved toward the volcano again. I had only gone a few minutes when I heard a loud splash somewhere past the trees. Thinking it was some sort of monster, I decided to investigate— better to identify threats than ignore them. To my immense relief, I saw Nessa!

She seemed to have fallen into a stream, and a giant dragon-thing with no front legs loomed over her, its back to me. A wyvern.

The wyvern lunged toward her. I shot a Fulminum spell and struck the wyvern right where its neck joined its head.

Smoke came out of the wyvern's mouth, and it keeled over, its scales going gray.

Nessa leaped out of the stream and ran to me.

"Nice spell casting! We've been so worried, Khi! Are you okay? Those portalic brambles teleported you, didn't they? They teleported everything in their vicinity to random places, including Max and me." She examined me, trying to gauge my health. I was pretty disheveled from all the warlocks and demons and running and puddles and birds and spiders and breaking branches, my pants ripped and my robe torn since I had forgotten to conjure new clothes after fighting Hebïra. Nessa's clothes, on the other hand, looked freshly washed. She wasn't even wet from the stream, and her hair was perfect. She had to teach me how to do that. She also didn't seem bothered or even grateful about the wyvern. I guess she could have handled that on her own.

"I'm fine. I met a warlock and a demon after that," I said with a grin. I had been scared going up against the monsters, but now that I had escaped, I felt kinda proud. Nessa's eyebrows shot up. "Oh, great gods. Are you okay?"

"I'm fine," I said.

"All I met was that wyvern," said Nessa. "I thought it was a green, blob-shaped fruit on a bush, but then it grew into a monster!" Wait. Was the green blob that bit me and broke the hypnotism . . . a wyvern?

I told her the story—when I mentioned Hebïra's transformation into a bloodthirsty monster, Nessa folded her arms and pursed her lips.

We set up camp a little way down from the stream, in a clearing. Nessa conjured a tent and two mattresses. Once again, she drew a circle of symbols around it for protection.

I decided not to go exploring this time. The Wildlandes were a bit too dangerous.

CHAPTER 14

Angeline

NESSA BATHED IN THE STREAM WHERE the wyvern had been—better than wasting magic to conjure water. She sterilized the stream, though, and conjured soap.

I bathed after her. It wasn't terrible, as streams go. Thankfully, there were no dead wyvern parts in it; Nessa had put them all in her magical locker for anatomical study.

Partway through my bath, the stream filled with these weird, black fish with no eyes. They unnerved me, but since they got through Nessa's runic shield, they were probably safe. Still, the idea of touching a slimy fish was enough to cut my bath short.

As I came back to camp, I heard a stifled gasp and rustling in some bushes next to me.

"Who's there?" I said. Considering I had just been bathing naked in a stream, the idea of someone hiding in the bushes didn't seem pleasant at all—oh, and the fact that most living things in the Wildlandes were demons.

"Show yourself," I said.

A girl crept out from the bushes. She had platinum blonde hair and huge, innocent, green eyes. Her eyes were filled with apprehension and fear, yet she looked determined at the same time. She was my age, hunkered in a defensive stance and holding a big sword in front of her. The sword had symbols inscribed along the blade, and the cross guard held several colorful jewels.

But the strangest thing were her clothes. They were . . . American—a short skirt and a t-shirt saying, "Girls rule, boys drool." (That saying was so five years ago.) "Who are you?" she asked. "You're another demon, aren't you?"

"What? What do you mean?" I asked.

"Why do you have purple eyes? You're definitely a demon. Normal people don't have purple eyes!"

"Hey! Just because I've got purple eyes doesn't mean I'm a demon! Who are you anyway? Where did you come from?"

"Well, sorry if I mistook you for a demon," she said, her voice unsteady. "I've seen all sorts of demons that look like teenage boys with weird eyes! I'm from Cupertino. That's in California, a state in America. But I don't think I'm in America. Is this, like, Hell?"

I tried to calm down. "Well, my name is Khi, and I can see you're genuinely afraid of demons, so I assume you are human. Who are you?"

She sighed. "I'm Angeline-Marena. I usually go by Angeline."

"You have two names?" I asked.

"Well . . . not exactly. My dad, uh, wanted to name me Angeline and my mom wanted to name me Marena, so they kind of compromised."

I blinked. "Okay. What are you doing here? How are you still alive in the Wildlandes, presumably without magic?"

"You called this place the Wildlandes, right? I was biking from school and rode into this smoky fog. When I came out, my bike had melted into a mangled heap of metal and rubber, and then I fell into, like, a dark place, and then I was here. I just know that every monster I slice with this sword vaporizes. I found it stuck in the ground."

"Khi!" came a voice. It was Max. "I thought I'd never find you!"

"Max!" I gave him a big hug. "I found Nessa and set up camp with her! I'm sorry those brambles teleported everyone. You won't believe what I've been through! I met warlocks and demons!"

"You've got to tell me all about that," said Max. "Who's she?" He looked warily at Angeline.

"Max, this is Angeline. She's a nonmagical from . . . Cupertino, in California. She somehow ended up here. I think Triskén may have been involved. Angeline, this is Max, my best friend."

Max looked shocked. "You've survived in the Wildlandes without magic?"

He noticed the sword and his eyes widened. "Excalibur!"

"Excalibur?" said Angeline.

"The legendary sword of the earth, King Arthur's sword! Merlin's sword! One of the five lost holy swords of power! The swords have been missing since Merlin, the greatest wizard of all time, died in the Wildlandes! That sword returns things to their origins and undoes what has been done! It can't even be lifted except by one who is worthy of it."

"Wait, what?" said Angeline, looking even more confused.

At the same time, I said, "Wait, so Angeline is holding King Arthur's sword?"

I hadn't noticed it at first, but a wave of pungent magical smell hit me from the sword. I felt light-headed. It was magic.

Max said, "Your sword is legendary. It's magic."

"Whoa, whoa, whoa. Hold on. Magic is not real. It's just in fairy tales."

I snorted and gestured around us. "And all of this isn't magical? Don't deny it, you know it's true. You should come with us. We can protect you."

I winced, realizing I sounded like just about every evil person in a movie who tried to make a deal with a protagonist. Angeline thought for a moment and said, "Okay. I'll travel with you."

Suddenly, her expression became guarded, and she lifted the sword up. I turned to see Nessa.

"Oh, hey, Nessa."

"Khi . . . who is this?" The two girls gave each other wary looks.

"This is Angeline," I said. "She came from Vhestibulium by accident. I'm not sure how, but I feel like it might be connected to Triskén. I think we should help her get back to Earth. Also, she kind of, sort of, found the superpowered legendary sword of Merlin."

Nessa nodded, her eyes wide but still distrustful. I didn't get it—didn't Nessa have lie detection magic? Couldn't she see the super powerful sword in Angeline's hands?

Angeline followed us to camp, pestering us about why we were in the Wildlandes. We only gave her vague answers about it being an accident. Her pestering was annoying but also kind of cute. You know what . . . forget I said that. I didn't mean she was cute like . . . well, you know what I mean! I mean, okay yeah, she was pretty and all, but—okay, please, forget everything I just said.

Nessa magically summoned another tent for Angeline to sleep in. The next morning, we all cleared out of the way as Nessa did a spell that stored a rectangular-prism-shaped area of matter in her magical locker, which was apparently some sort of mystical interdimensional space where wizards could store things they wanted to access later without having to carry around bags. (I kind of tuned out the science babble—it was literally quantum physics!) All that was left of the camp were the weird symbols Nessa drew on the ground. Nessa waved her hand and most of them vanished, though a few became white paint and swirled into a bottle Nessa had conjured. I think she did it to annoy Angeline, who was standing close and yelped as the vacuum created by the vanishing matter pulled her in and spun her around.

"Holy mother of God!" she cried. "Where did everything go? And what was that wind?"

Nessa laughed, but I reprimanded her. Angeline was a Vhestibulian; she didn't know what magic was like, just like I hadn't when I first came to Elkloria.

"We should head for the volcano," said Nessa. "There's a lot of thermal energy in volcanoes—maybe I can convert that to fire magic and utilize it to find a way to get home."

We glided toward it on hoverboards made with our magic (we didn't go too high because of that smoky air problem I encountered before). The hoverboards wouldn't last forever and could only be conjured once an hour, so eventually, we'd have to walk again unless we could conjure magical steeds or something.

Angeline sat behind me while I stood and steered our hoverboard—Max had taught me how to enlarge it so multiple people could sit on it. Angeline, Max, and I traded stories about life in Vhestibulium. I liked hearing Angeline laugh. It was contagious. Nessa glided nearby, pretending to look disinterested but obviously listening in.

Eventually, we reached a wall—a long, long wall. Nessa said, "**Velexterna**," and a small, glowing sphere fluttered in her hand. It flew off into the distance, where the wall disappeared in the trees. Nessa's eyes had a sort of moving glow, like those loading icons with a spinning blue circle, or like radar. Her brow was furrowed in concentration. Of course! She was using the fluttering sphere as a third eye.

The glow in her eyes disappeared, and she blinked a few times. "This wall . . . ends, like, at the shore of the Wildlandes. Behind it is a maze. There's a sign at the entrance," she said. "It's the Temple of Zanzazia."

A vague memory tugged at my mind. "Zanzazia . . . Zanzazia was . . . the first demon queen, right?"

Nessa nodded. Angeline looked at us in confusion. "Let's go," Nessa said. "The entrance is this way."

We came across a large archway covered in red, glowing runes. They looked familiar, but I couldn't figure out why.

"I wonder what those runes say," I said.

"Where?" asked Nessa. "I can't see any runes."

"There," I pointed.

Nessa immediately realized. "Right. It's in, uh . . . that language I can read."

I looked up. Wow, the Wildlandes sky was really beautiful. Sure, it looked like something out of a painting of the Christian hell, all fiery and swirling, but it had this sun-surface glow that was really pretty.

164

I shook my head. Wasn't I talking to Nessa about something?

"What were we talking about?" I said.

Nessa gave me a strange look. "The temple of Zanzazia."

Had someone cast some kind of distraction spell? Angeline looked at us in bewilderment. Did she cast the spell? No, of course not. Nessa? Maybe she had been lying before, but about what? I shook my head and decided not to mention my confusion. The others would probably think I was crazy.

We walked into the maze. Nessa pointed to the left fork. Max conjured a glowing trail behind us. As we followed the twisting paths of the maze, Nessa muttered spell words over and over. Sweat appeared on her forehead, but nothing else happened. Max seemed to be doing the same thing.

"What's wrong?" I asked.

Nessa frowned. "I've been trying to cast motion spells to get us through, destruction spells to break down the walls, location spells to find the end of the maze, even a simple Velexterna spell to see the maze. But nothing's working, even though my magic feels invigorated."

Max nodded. "Same for me. Nothing works, except for that illusion trail spell I cast."

"It's like the maze is forbidding us from using spells. Ugh, it's like those maze games I used to play back with my friends—they had enchantments to prevent me from cheating. Someone or something wants us to go through this maze the long way. Max's illusion trail probably only works because it doesn't allow us to cheat on the maze."

I frowned. "I guess we've got to do this the hard way."

"Well . . . I'm pretty good at mazes," said Angeline.

Nessa raised an eyebrow. "Actual mazes? I don't mean to be rude, but real ones are way harder than mazes on paper."

Angeline looked at her feet. "I know. Just a random thought. Anyway, Max made a path behind us, like the spool of thread Ariadne gave Theseus in the Greek myth. I think it'll be pretty easy to get through."

Nessa frowned. "Ariadne? Like the goddess of maps?"

I raised my eyebrows. "Wait, what?" I said as Angeline said, "Goddess?"

Nessa shook her head. "Never mind. But seriously, Angeline, solving this maze will not be a simple task. Magical mazes could have all sorts of unexpected and unpredictable things that you'd never find in some simple Vhestibulian puzzle maze."

I looked at Nessa crossly. "Nessa, you shouldn't be rude to Angeline. Just because she's Vhestibulian and doesn't know about magic doesn't mean you should look down on her."

"That's not why . . . I'm not trying to . . . " Nessa trailed off, looking ashamed.

As we were talking, we turned a corner and came face to face with a minotaur.

Angeline's eyes went saucer wide. She clutched my arm. For a second, I felt a happy little tingle that she ran to *me* for protection. It passed as I realized there was, well, a minotaur in front of us. Angeline held her sword out with her free hand.

Nessa glared at the sword. What was that about?

The minotaur raised its axe. It was about to bring it down on Nessa when she shot a spell at it, and the minotaur disappeared in a blue flash. I made a mental note of that spell—it seemed useful.

Well, that was easy. Was the minotaur that weak or was Nessa that powerful? She could copy spells, she had technomagy—which no one else had, or everyone who *had* it couldn't use it anymore because they were darkins or whatever—she had omni-magic, two forms . . .

What kept her from being, well, basically a goddess? If she wasn't such a good person, she could conquer the world. Or if Triskén got its hands (or vaporous tentacles) on her, it could use her as a powerful weapon. While I was thinking about all this, Angeline led us to a door in another archway surrounded by symbols. Angeline pushed it open.

CHAPTER 15

Spectral

SEVERAL NOISES CAME FROM THE OTHER side—people yelling, a raspy breathing, the tsss-BOOM of magic. I dashed inside and saw Korukan, Metara, Lianaka, and another boy I didn't know fighting something I couldn't see. All manner of colorful spells flew back and forth. Whatever they fought shifted like heat distortion, except it cast a very faint shadow on the ground. Metara tried an ectomagical spell that should have worked on intangible beings. It went right through with no effect.

Lianaka created an assortment of illusions and sent them to attack. (I got a feeling they were illusions—they were so seamless that only my magic sense could tell me they weren't real.) Maybe she thought intangible illusions could hit the creature, but they too did nothing. The boy I didn't know clutched a gold chain around his neck, conjuring all sorts of objects to fling at the enemy. Uselessly—they passed right through it.

Korukan shot a spell through the ghostly being, hitting the wall of the maze and covering it in a giant sheet of reflective glass shimmering with faint blue light. In the glass, I could see the being clearly—a black frayed robe with two blue eyes under the hood.

"A specter," said Nessa.

Its eyes had turned toward us in the mirror. It glided toward me then right through me! My chest felt like it was full of ice water. I collapsed, coughing.

The specter moved toward Nessa next. Angeline stood petrified. Now my chest burned as if I had spilled hot water on myself. My thoughts became sluggish. With all my willpower, I shouted, "Angeline! Excalibur! Use it on the specter!" I didn't know what Excalibur would do, but it was one of the most powerful magical relics in the world. It had to do something.

Angeline looked at me in horror. Then she looked at the sword and back at the specter that was gliding toward us. Nessa lay on the ground shivering. I found the others, and they were all down too—slumped against walls or laying on top of one another. Angeline was the only person left standing.

The specter looked at her. Her eyes hardened with determination as it glided toward her, and she swung the sword. It connected with a flash! The specter glowed brighter and brighter, until it evaporated into nothing. I smiled wearily, so did the others—all except Nessa, who was frowning at where the specter had been. She looked distrustfully at Angeline.

I fainted then; the last thing I saw was Angeline looking horror-struck as my head hit the ground.

⚜ ⚜ ⚜

I SLOWLY CAME TO. I WAS in the same place, but I was lying on my back now. Angeline was awake, sitting near us and looking at the sky, sword in her hand. The others were laid out in a row next to me, still unconscious.

Angeline smiled at me. "You're awake!"

"How long was I out?"

Angeline shrugged. "An hour or so."

She pulled me up. I thanked her and looked at the others. Nessa stirred, then woke first. We both smiled at her.

"How was your sleep, Nessa?" asked Angeline.

"Fine . . . " Nessa said, still looking at Angeline distrustfully.

"Nessa . . . " I said, "Angeline, can you excuse us for a minute?"

Angeline nodded, and Nessa and I walked out into a maze corridor.

I got straight to the point. "Why don't you like Angeline? Is this . . . I dunno . . . prejudice? Because she's from Vhestibulium?"

Nessa shook her head. "No, it's just . . . It doesn't add

up. Why would a random girl, who just happened to appear in the Wildlandes, be able to wield Excalibur, the legendary sword of the origins? It's supposed to be usable only by those with the most noble intentions, but all she was trying to do was survive. And . . . I'm not sure her sword is returning things to their origins. Specters are people under a certain curse, so the specter should have turned into a person . . . "

I sighed, exasperated. Angeline was a good person. She had saved us all from the specter. Nessa's attitude made me mad.

"And the sword," she said. "At first I thought it was covered in symbols, but it just has words like 'Excalibur,' 'Caliburn,' and 'Origin' written in really fancy cursive."

I was taken aback. This was a new low for Nessa. "I've only ever seen symbols on it," I said coldly.

Nessa frowned. "But . . . Could it be in the demonic language I can understand?"

"Why would Excalibur have demonic symbols on it?"

"Maybe it isn't Excalibur."

"I think you're jealous because the sword chose a non-magical girl instead of a powerful wizard like you. And the symbols . . . maybe it's some other arcane magic language you happen to know."

My logical mind told me I should have been suspicious of Angeline—or at least of the sword. But Angeline didn't deserve to be treated the way Nessa was treating her.

Nessa looked down at her feet. "I'm sorry. I'm just making up excuses to distrust her. It's just . . . I don't like trusting people because . . . "

Her eyes glistened. Suddenly, she was crying, shuddering without sound. Surprised, I felt guilty about how I had treated her. I put my arms around her and let her cry into my shoulder for a little while.

"Nessa?" I asked quietly. "Do you want to talk about it?"

She sniffed. "I'm . . . Khi, you may think I'm a super cool sister. But you're as wrong as you can get. You know why I'm so touchy about trusting Angeline? Our relatives, besides you and my parents . . . they hate my guts. If my relatives hate me, a random girl will not just suddenly like me. When I was twelve, Lady Velyne actually tried to have me poisoned. She was taken to the dungeons, and my parents tried to hide it from me, but I knew she had poisoned my drink, I knew the petals she put in the drink hadn't belonged to roses, but to the deadly mortal umbra flower. I frequently thanked the gods that she didn't have magic for two months after that. And Lord Avilum tried to push me out a window! Twenty-three stories up!

"After that, Mom, Dad, and I rarely went to family gatherings. My parents said Lord Avilum was just clumsy and knocked into me, but I knew better. And then there was Ashbir, my best friend and the only noble I trusted . . . He never tried to kill me, thank the gods, but now he hates me, too. I don't even know why. But the problem isn't them anymore. My heart stopped taking betrayals a

long time ago. The attempted murders, and even the
little things, the words, glares, subtle hints of pure hatred,
from relatives, from kids at school. They can't hurt me
anymore. Not even poison could! My magic is just too
powerful!" She laughed hysterically, as if broken inside
and out.

"The problem is me! All of it still affects me, even if I
can protect myself. I still flinch when one of my relatives
walks toward me. And Khi, I'm sorry. I tried to hide this
from you, but look at me—crying to you, making you
worried, when we have so much to worry about right now.
I should be dealing with this alone, so we can deal with
the problem of being stuck in the Wildlandes, but my
stupid emotions got in the way! I'm just jealous. I guess I
deserve it . . . "

I was shocked at what I was hearing.

People had tried to murder Nessa.

Not only that, but Nessa hated herself. And the only
people she trusted were her parents, Sir Korukan, and
Lianaka, whom she had been with from childhood. For
her friends from the royal academy, she put up a facade
of having a perfect princess life, never letting them see
her pain, her dark secrets. Even her friends at the
academy were few. So many kids at school judged her
right away, shunning her and bullying her. Metara and
Max . . . She liked them, but eventually, her facade would
crack, and they would see how horrible she was. Even
Ashbir had betrayed her. Why should she trust a random

girl in the Wildlandes carrying a sword that was so obviously demonic in nature? Her own relatives had tried to kill her!

Wait, what? These weren't my thoughts . . . Nessa's thoughts were spilling into my mind without her realizing it—like accidental telepathy.

"Nessa . . . why don't they like you?" I said tentatively. Something seemed off.

Quietly, she said, "I don't . . . know."

Was she lying? Did the nobles know something she didn't? From what I knew, Nessa was a great person. Why would people not like her?

"Why do you trust me, if you don't trust anyone?"

Nessa's face was pale. "I suppose you're a trust-inducing demon. I can't help but tell you things I've only told my parents and Lianaka. It's scary . . . and yet, it's relieving. And . . . you're just so easy to trust, even for someone like me. That is a dangerous quality . . . but it can also be a good one—as long as it doesn't result in my demise. And I know you. You're my brother. Whether or not you were nearly a stranger when I first met you, we had a connection. My parents went to great lengths to make you the amazing person you are today, including having the two people they trusted most be your parents in Vhestibulium. But Angeline . . . I don't know her, and I have no reason to trust her. She could be anyone, from anywhere. She could be lying, and I'd never know because she might just have powerful magic."

THE DOOR TO INFERNA

Quietly, I said, "I'll never betray you. But Nessa . . . Angeline. She's done nothing but help us all this time. She killed the specter, remember? And she watched over us while we slept. Give her a chance."

Nessa looked at me. "I suppose it's my suspicious nature. Angeline just . . . appeared out of the Wildlandes, holding a powerful magical weapon . . . You guys became friends so quickly. It seemed too convenient, and the Vhestibulium story so far-fetched. Her eyes seemed so innocent that it made me angry. The kids at school who judged me, the relatives who tried to kill me . . . they all acted innocent. But I guess that's stupid, isn't it? If they looked suspicious, I still wouldn't have trusted them. I guess I've got to teach myself that not everyone is against me. I'll try to trust Angeline. She is a good person."

I smiled at her. "How about after this Wildlandes mission you come to Vhestibulium with me? See what it's like there. Live life there for a little while."

Nessa looked interested but apprehensive. "If it's no trouble . . . "

"I'm sure my adoptive parents would love to have you. And so would I!"

She finally smiled. "Okay. But that's a promise now, and you better keep it. I guess it's true, 'the intelligent man divides his work with his wife.'"

I shook my head. "Uh . . . what?"

Nessa laughed. "Oh, right. It's an Elklorian saying. It means the best way to relieve a burden is to share it with another. Thanks for listening to me. There aren't a lot of people I've had the courage to tell this to."

I smiled and hugged her again. "You're quite welcome."

A thought came to my mind—what if she had unknowingly committed a crime? A crime . . . of her birth? What if her whole family knew of something dark inside her, and she was the only one who didn't know?

Hopefully, Nessa didn't notice my smile falter.

We walked back to the others. Metara and Korukan were waking up. Lia and the boy I didn't know were still unconscious.

Metara took one look at Max, threw herself into his arms, and hugged him so hard his face turned blue. "Are you okay? I was so worried!"

She stepped back. "You look pretty healthy . . . Can I do an emotional scan on you?"

Korukan gave us a haggard look. He growled, "Do you have any idea how worried you made us, Princess Prissy? Disappearing? Confronting the cult of Ex Morte by yourself?"

I winced. "It wasn't her fault. I suggested we go to a restaurant to clear our thoughts and it happened to be where the Ex Morte cult was. They kind of kidnapped us. Wait, how did you know that's where we were? And how did you get here?"

Korukan said, "Nessa's NOTT communicator sent out a distress call before we lost the signal behind some sort of magic nullification field. There was neuronoxine in her veins. We tracked the call, but then you disappeared through that peculiar doorway. Your communicator pinged again while you were in the warp zone between the cult location and the Wildlandes. We couldn't teleport to you due to saltwater, so we came by ship. Thankfully, the firestorm was gone. Do you know how you got here? It shouldn't be possible."

Nessa shrugged. "I have no clue. Saltwater dampens teleportation almost completely. The only way I can think of that one might get around that rule is god-level magic power."

Lianaka and the boy stirred. The boy had wavy brown hair and crystal blue eyes. He wore a gold necklace and a blue robe. Lianaka wore a solid blue dress with a white capelet that had a green brooch on it.

Lia blinked and looked at Nessa. Her eyes widened, and she, too, ran and squeezed Nessa tightly.

Then she put her fingers on Nessa's forehead and said, "You feel happy, and you look healthy."

Suddenly, her eyes flashed. "Why the Inferna did you take on the Ex Morte cult by yourself?!"

Nessa looked scared. Feeling the need to defend her again, I said, "It was an accident. I mean, it was unintentional. I don't know if it was an accident. Nessa and I went to clear our heads, and the cult was there."

Lia's scary stare turned to me. I shrank away, but then the intensity in her eyes lessened. "I doubt it was an accident. The Ex Morte cult wouldn't kidnap you for no reason. Well, at least the Ex Morte cult was arrested and the entire alterspace of the kingdom was searched, so Neurazia is probably safe again. But Nessa has a history of sneaking out to buy interesting things and getting tangled up with muggers . . . I hope you can see why I was worried."

I was shocked at the thought of Nessa fighting muggers. As to sneaking out in the first place . . . well, it actually sounded kind of like her.

The boy with brown hair stood off to the side, smiling. Korukan noticed me looking at him. "Oh! I forgot to introduce you. Khi, this is a new NOTT recruit, Furorde. He's the one with the demonic amulet I told you about— a cursed necklace that gives him power. I decided that since the prophecy mentions a 'demon child,' it might be better to bring one of our own, in this case Furorde, so that we can make sure the demon child is good and Fate doesn't have to introduce an evil demon child into our destinies."

I wasn't sure how that made sense, but I shook Furorde's hand. Korukan continued, "Nimori will be a lunar eclipse, or blood moon, the night after tomorrow. Khi's prophecy mentioned Lunella, and while the prophecy's verbs were debatable, I believe we should monitor the demon portal until the end of the blood moon to ensure that, if the darkins have some other way to open the portal—perhaps another sacrifice— they cannot open it."

"Where is the portal?" I asked.

Lia pointed to the enormous volcano looming above us. "In the crater."

⚜ ⚜ ⚜

WE ALL KNEW WE NEEDED TO send Angeline back to Neurazia or Earth to protect her from what was coming, but no one knew how. Nessa said both her normal and transdimensional teleporter didn't work from unmapped areas like the Wildlandes. But then Korukan suggested that since the maze was really close to the portal, the transdimensional energy from the portal could help boost the teleporter's ability to open a portal across universes. Korukan was correct—the transdimensional teleporter successfully opened a doorway to an alley near Angeline's house.

Angeline and I had grown kind of close, and she refused to let her memories of magic be erased—and since erasing memories without consent was illegal under Elklorian law, her memories remained intact. However, a forceful no-speaking spell was put on her so she couldn't mention Elkloria to others—more for her own safety than ours. If she talked about magic and demons, people would think she was crazy.

"Goodbye, Khi. I hope we meet again." As Angeline was about to leave, she leaned over and kissed me on the cheek. The portal closed behind her, and I stared into the space where it had been, my face redder than a firetruck, my mouth hanging open.

"By the gods, Khi," said Nessa, "you've already enamored two people—you're quite a player!"

I collected myself and punched her lightly. Max had a faintly jealous look on his face that made me feel very self-conscious.

When she had gone, we continued out of the maze. The dark forest ahead of us was eerily silent.

CHAPTER 16

Tãnayapédémônia

WE REACHED THE FOOT OF THE volcano the evening before the blood moon. The volcano rose high above us into the igniferous sky. The atmosphere was dry as . . . not dirt, but . . . sand. That's it. Desert sand. It was nowhere near the cool, sweet air of Elkloria. It was thin and made my throat feel scratchy all the time.

We'd need devices or amulets of some kind for air. Nessa conjured these handy tanks and helmets (well, she conjured a bunch of pieces that attached together to make the devices). She said they'd provide air for hours. She also said she could conjure air with magic if necessary, or if she wasn't available (not a pleasant thought), then the transdimensional teleporter could open a rift to Vhestibulium to provide breathable air. It could also be used to escape if the need arose.

Nessa and I changed to our dragon forms (to the surprise of Metara) and carried the others to a ledge near the top.

Having people on my back was not very pleasant. Dragon scales have sensitive nerves, and I could feel their every movement. It was distracting. Not to mention when they stretched and whacked my wings or something by mistake, it threw me off balance. I did not want to carry anyone else in the future, even though I probably would at some point—flight transportation is pretty useful. Maybe real dragons were better at it, but I was still new.

The ledge sat underneath a bunch of bushes and trees. (Somehow, they could grow on the side of a volcano—super-plants, huh?) Nessa used her Velexterna spell to see what was above us. This time, a magical screen showed us what her spell saw, with little glowing circles that controlled the spell, so we could move the "camera" around like a spy drone. It showed an enormous crater that extended down into a pit of magma, bright red with streaks and patches of black rock. The magma swirled rapidly in a fiery orange whirlpool with a brightly glowing center—so bright I couldn't make out anything in it.

Above the magma whirlpool, I saw a kind of rippling film—like cellophane, except electricity flickered across its surface. Sequences of magical symbols, geometric shapes, and weird equations appeared and disappeared, wiggling all over its surface like ghostly sea snakes in a time lapse. They followed a vaguely spiral-shaped path.

Where the film touched the walls of the volcano, there was a glowing border, uneven and broken.

I tore my eyes from the magical seal and noticed thirteen people in hoods around the crater. Through the spy-spell screen's invisible speakers I heard them chanting *"Tãnayapédêmônia"* over and over again. Definitely not Phantasian.

Nessa said, so quietly that I was sure only I could hear, "They're saying, 'Open, demonic portal.' But I thought they needed to sacrifice a loved one."

I turned to her. "How . . . did you understand that?"

She seemed not to hear me. "What if they do open the portal? Will we need a sacrifice to close it?"

I watched the hooded figures on the screen, wondering whether Nessa ignored my questions or hadn't heard. Though, the last thing she said had me thinking. What happened to the sacrifice?

There were now twenty-six hooded figures. Each of the thirteen new arrivals (where had they even come from?) threw an oily, black stone into the portal seal.

Korukan said, "The darkins' magic is causing the seal to decay. Before the darkins' curse, only minor mortal demons could get through the seal. There are three types of demons. Mortal demons can die like normal creatures. They are the most diverse group—as diverse as the kingdoms of life. Half-mortal demons are more rare. They are more powerful than mortal demons and have a human aspect and a creature aspect, resulting in a sort of hybrid form. Half-mortal demons are strange because they reincarnate in their birth place when killed—or as close to it as their infernal hearts can reach.

"Then, there are the immortal demons, the most powerful, on par with the Fae. They greatly dwarf the other demons in power—and almost every being that exists— and they cannot die. They should not get out. Ever. As the seal decays, more powerful demons will be able to get through, but immortal demons will only get through if the seal breaks completely—with a sacrifice, we hypothesized. We must, however, assume that the portal can open without a sacrifice because we do not know for sure, and must proceed to stop this ceremony. We must not let the darkins capture us, because, aside from the fact we want to protect our lives, if a sacrifice is really required for the portal, we must not give it to them. So, here's the plan. We'll hide ourselves amongst this volcano's strange vegetation.

"When I give the signal, we will slip out of our hiding spots along the edges of the crater and knock out darkins with the Nocolco spell. Using magic to hide ourselves is a bad idea—they will probably smell it. In fact, we shouldn't use magic until we reveal ourselves."

We climbed up the side of the volcano using indentations in the rock. My arms and legs ached. Then, we hid in different areas of the underbrush as quietly as possible. In the bushes across the crater from me, Korukan held up his hand.

His hand became a closed fist, and I leapt out of the bushes, casting the Nocolco spell twice to knock out the darkins in front of me.

The others knocked out their darkins with flashes of cyan. But one of the darkins managed to escape. He cried out, "*øTānayapêdävda, gad Sôsäxtaxxilriar,*" when a bolt of energy slammed into him.

He was knocked unconscious by the spell bolt. A piece of black stone skittered from his hand, falling into the mouth of the volcano before anyone could stop it. The rippling seal ruptured, spilling white light. We watched in horror as the rupture grew bigger and bigger. It began sucking in everything around it. I grabbed a nearby tree just as my feet left the ground. My body waved like a flag in the wind, straining against the sucking vortex. My already-aching arms screamed. The fiery clouds above, purple like an evening sky, formed a funnel, swirling into the rupture. Unconscious darkins and pieces of black stone were pulled in, and I think someone's shoes went flying in too. Leaves swirled. Rocks flew.

It was all I could do to cling to the tree.

"The portal doesn't need a sacrifice?" I yelled.

Nessa yelled back, "I don't think it's fully opened yet! The portal is already shrinking! I'm pretty sure the darkin simply started the process. It will reseal itself!" My fingers slipped. I couldn't hold on any longer. Just as I was about to let go of the tree, the sucking stopped.

Everything was calm for a moment. Then clouds shot out of the portal along with darkin bodies, stones, dirt, leaves, and a pair of shoes. The shimmering seal now had a large crack down the middle, dark smoke issuing from it. Shards of black stone rained down, but a strange purple-and-black shield protected us. I didn't have time to wonder about that, because several demons shot out of the portal at the same time.

"That's a half-mortal demon!" yelled Korukan, pointing at a spider with a woman's upper body where its head should be. "Pair up! It has the power of two wizards!"

The spider woman landed on the edge of the crater, causing a shockwave to shake the area and cracks to appear in the dirt. Six snakes with golden horns floated in the air around her. She opened her mouth to reveal two hideous, clicking mandibles. The woman hissed and leaped at me.

My eyes popped wide in terror. I couldn't move.

Korukan yelled, "**Dispul Dileferris**."

The spell hit the demon. She froze in place then fell to the ground, blue flames exploding on her back. The flames vanished and she returned to her feet.

"It will take two of us," Korukan said to me. "This spell sends demons back to Inferna. Help me!"

Korukan held his hand out and shot the spell again, visibly straining against some invisible force, curving his fingers as the blue fire crept up the demon's body. The demon struggled to break free of the fire's hold. She

THE DOOR TO INFERNA

managed to move closer to me, but I had regained my wits and shot my own Dispul Dileferris. Under our combined force, the demon disappeared in a flash of blue. Korukan and I grinned at each other.

Suddenly, one of the horned demon snakes flew at Korukan. Another flew at me, but Metara appeared in a blur, creating a shield just as the snake blew white-hot fire at us. Metara cast a bright spell that sent the demon flying back into the crater. It landed on top of the rippling portal, now just a bubbling, hissing carcass.

Soon enough, all the flying snakes were smoking carcasses or vaporized from the heat of the lava.

A glowing light shone from the crater. The seal began reforming. Electric snakes made of symbols and equations consumed each other, becoming longer equations.

We all cheered as, gradually, the hole in the seal shrank.

Korukan patted me on the back and said, "Good job!"

Metara, Max, and Nessa did a group high five. Lia gave Furorde a big hug.

The dark clouds gathered above. Purple lightning sliced down from the clouds and struck the seal, causing small holes to appear.

Nessa tilted her head and said, "That doesn't look good . . . "

The clouds swirled into the form of a giant woman with gray skin, long black hair, and glowing purple eyes. She floated above the seal.

"Hello, Khioneus, Khyonessa! We meet again. And, oh, you have a squad now!" Its voice had an undertone like sharp wind and a crackle like static.

Triskén.

"Why did you have to come?" I whispered.

Purple lightning continued to strike the seal. Tentacles of dark smoke swirled around her and uprooted trees, dropping them into the portal.

One of the tentacles swooped down and grabbed me. I flew through the air. Wind blew fast, and my robes flapped, slapping me in the face. I kicked and screamed. I tried every spell I knew. Nothing had any effect.

I didn't want to die! Not like this. Not bringing about the end of all that existed.

"LET GO OF HIM!" cried Metara.

Triskén smiled widely. "No chance of that. The portal will open once it's sucked out all of Khioneus's magic. Once a wizard loses all his magic, he dies. Khioneus will die to open the portal and shall be my sacrifice of love."

Max, Metara, and Nessa screamed, "NO!"

Lia, Korukan, and Furorde stood horrified.

Triskén's head floated near me and whispered, "It'll be fun torturing your friends while you suffer. But you won't die. I was sure you had infinite magic power, and the cult did their job confirming my hypothesis. Remember in the Ex Morte hideout, when the cage you were in shattered? You overloaded your extractor an hour after they started extracting with all that magic of yours. And with your infinite magic, I can keep the portal open forever."

"What?" I said. "What do you mean?"

"I think you know what I mean." Triskén laughed. "Look at those friends of yours, Khioneus. Look how much love you've gathered. Isn't it terrible you'll never see your loved ones again? The demons will kill them all. And they'll never know that you'll still be alive after the portal opens."

"They'll stop you," I said, unconvinced by my own bluster.

Triskén vanished. I floated above the portal. A shaft of light shone from the seal and held me in place. Cyan swirls of magic flowed around me and down the shaft in double helices, and, as my magic left me, I began to feel sick. My head was seized with a splitting headache and my stomach felt empty. I struggled to breathe, and my muscles burned with lactic acid as they got less oxygen. A hole in the portal widened. The seal began burning away.

A wave of potent and powerful dark magic—which would have knocked me over with its dead-fish smell, if I hadn't been paralyzed—came from the seal below. Then the seal was gone. Trapped with a pounding head, I was unable to grasp what it meant to have infinite magic. Had Triskén thought I'd already known?

Something burst out of the portal—a blurred geyser of red below me. And I knew—either from the immense magic power or the feeling of extreme terror—that an immortal demon had entered the world.

He floated beneath me. He was gigantic, with red skin and muscular arms. His armor seemed to drip crimson with blood. Dark hair hung to his shoulders. His horns were small, but his glowing wings—shimmering with enchantments or curses—were enormous. He might have been handsome by Earth standards if not for the sinister smile on his fanged lips and eyes that looked like dark holes.

"Humans," he hissed. His voice was smooth and melodic, like a song played in a minor key. It terrified me. "General Zarqin will be happy to learn the portal is open. And if I destroy the defenses of this planet, perhaps even a lowly servant such as I will be promoted. The other immortal demons have grown lazy, paying no attention to the Tempestuous Desert on our planet. I hope to keep it that way until I've conquered this world for my superiors. Yes . . . perhaps I can even become general. General Gonzäro! A nice ring to it, that is for sure."

"Holy Ravilux," Korukan said weakly. "May the god Destinis of fate help us."

The demon smirked at Korukan. "But Destinis is simply a god. The gods are nothing compared to the power of an immortal demon—not even your silly god of fate. Mortals believe fate is undeniable, but we know fate is simply a nuisance, able to be bent and stretched as we see fit. And you, Khioneus Nevula, are at my mercy, as are your friends. Nothing can stop me—not even fate. Your fate . . . is mine."

A tendril of red magic grabbed me. The paralysis broke, but I fell limp, too tired to move. The portal didn't kill me. Did I have infinite magic like Triskén said? But why?

Max cried out, "You killed him! **Heliolumina Magna!**"

No, I thought. *I'm not dead! Stop talking! You'll provoke him!*

The spell flew right through Gonzäro's form.

Gonzäro said, "Well, I know who I will kill next."

"No!" I whispered, but it was too late. Light flashed around Max. His eyes widened, then closed. He fell to the ground with a thump.

I screamed, then realized that I could move.

Gonzäro smiled in satisfaction. Tears flowed from my eyes, floating in the air around me.

"You'll pay for that," I yelled. My voice echoed through the crater.

I heard gasps as people heard me and realized I was alive.

I was barely able to think through the haze of emotions and pain. I am sure I had forgotten how to think. Gonzäro looked down at me.

"Ah, an undead sacrifice. You should be dead, shouldn't you?" He sounded intrigued. "What are you? A wizard can only open the demon portal by giving up his life. I don't suppose it matters. You can't stop me. We are beings of magical energy, the most powerful thing in the universe. I can do anything I want, anything I can imagine, and you can't stop me. You should see the higher-ups in the immortal demons' hierarchy. You think I am powerful? I'm nothing compared to them."

His voice became resentful at that part, but then regained its delighted, evilly smug tone. "Perhaps I'll bring you back to life and kill you again for the fun of it. It will be so much fun seeing your bloody internal organs when I rip you open."

Then, through my haze of grief and anger, something pricked my mind. The fact that I wasn't dead was strange enough, but I remembered something Metara had said days ago: A Semideus is a holy magical being with capacities beyond those of a normal wizard—like prophesying, infinite magic power, the ability to neutralize all magic, and the power to turn into a god.

I had spoken a prophecy.

At the Temple of Azatalan, the dark unicorn's curse had broken the instant it touched me. Piece of evidence number two—the ability to neutralize all magic.

The demon portal was supposed to have sucked all the magic out of me and killed me, but I wasn't dead. Triskén had told me I wouldn't die, that it knew I had infinite magic, that it had sent the Ex Morte cult to confirm that. Triskén knew what I was. That was why Triskén wanted me to join it. It knew that with my infinite magic power, I would be able to keep the portal open. Max was never the sacrifice. Triskén had been trying to lure me all along.

I would have thought I was crazy if I was thinking straight, but the only thing I could think was that Max was dead—not because of Gonzäro, but because in his grief over what he thought was my death, he tried to avenge me. That was all that mattered.

I was a Semideus. I had to close the portal by changing into my divine form. A Semideus can bring back the dead, right?

"I'm gonna make you pay," I said, tears streaming from my eyes. Gonzäro raised his demonic eyebrows.

I knew what I needed to say. The words came to my head like a near-forgotten memory. "**Maethaea Nymfarannus.**"

The spell sounded like a dark curse the way I said it—with a fire of vengeance. Gonzäro was the reason Max was dead. He didn't deserve to exist in a world where Max had once lived.

Everything stopped moving. People froze in poses as a shockwave of energy rippled from me, swaying trees and blowing up dirt, with a sound like a colossal shotgun. My friends' eyes still moved, but that was it. Even Gonzäro was paralyzed. Trees combusted as I rose from the crater, transcending from my mortal form into something else, a storm of magic energy. The next thing I knew, I was looking down on everyone.

My mind was in a haze, consumed by grief. My clothes had combusted from the heat of my transformation, but I didn't have a form anymore. Some part of me found this problematic, and so my essence coalesced into a body. I was now wearing a blue tunic with gold trim. It was long, cinched by a belt at my waist, with flowing pants underneath. My eyes glowed brightly, and my skin was paper white, my hair silver. My ears were long and pointed, and my fingers were long and thin. I had a long, glowing tail and shimmering angel wings, and my feet were wreathed in white hot fire.

My mind wasn't in control of my new body. It was like the real me was trapped in a psychic cell. I could only watch as my anger and sadness came to life and controlled me. Because my new body was made of some kind of holy energy, the demonic energy of the Wildlandes burned my body, causing an almost unreal pain, but I didn't care.

My essence permeated the Wildlandes, cramped and straining to break free. If I could do that, my essence would spread to the many universes of the Aedis (I didn't know what that word actually meant but inexplicably knew it), bursting outward to create more worlds, more universes. I knew I could manifest anywhere within the Wildlandes that I wanted—even many places at once. I could see 360 degrees around me, through everything, inside everything. When I try to recall what I had seen, I can't—simply because my human brain is overwhelmed by this extra-dimensional sight. I saw universes full of strange creatures and planets and landscapes, universes that resided within the thoughts and feelings of people, and a universe where time was space.

I could see through the firestorm covering the sky, through Pyrhithya's solar system. I saw Max's soul being guided to the Luminous Netherworld (I knew its name even though I had never heard of it before) on a frozen planet at the edge of Pyrhithya's solar system. He was led by a Death Reaper—a winged boy wearing a loincloth and carrying a sword at his waist, flying toward the frozen planet of death almost at the speed of light. I grabbed Max's formless soul with psychic hands, pulling it through the vast expanse of space to his body lying at the bottom of the mountain. I lifted Max to the top of the mountain. Time resumed, everyone unfroze, and Max came back to life, gasping and looking dazed.

Gonzäro looked at me in confusion.

In fluent Phantasian, I said, *"Vokamupkhavadi ka savadi macremnamouz kameta calois ka darizeitouzavadi."*

I told you that you'd pay for what you've done.

I wasn't a god, I was a Fae, one of the most powerful beings in the known universes.

My rage was painful and fiery—the rage of a storm, a hurricane, an earthquake, a supernova. A rage that could bring about the end of the universe—of all the universes in the Aedis.

A small flame of darkness burned inside me. It whispered to let it take control. It told me how it would torture Gonzäro and show the demon why he should never mess with me. The anger toward Gonzäro was seeded in me. It wanted to grow.

My other emotions shut off completely. Rage was all that mattered. My friends told me later that my eyes turned solid white.

I shot a burst of blue light at Gonzäro. The burst was fueled by the flame of darkness that slowly grew inside me, telling me about all the ways I could make the demons pay for the crimes they committed, for what they did to Max.

The demon retaliated by shooting a sphere of darkness at me. I held up my hand and the volatile energy was teleported into an empty universe two miles away from this one. The demon shot a blast of red light. This attack caught me blindsided. It stung, but I ignored it and shot an even more powerful spell back, an inferno of blue fire. Gonzäro lost his focus and he transformed into a swirling black cloud with flashes of red energy.

This time I cast a spell that became a glowing net and wrapped around Gonzäro's nebulous form, condensing him into an oily black ball and dropping him into the volcanic portal. I heard a psychic scream of rage as he was propelled into the fiery depths of Inferna.

But I knew that he wouldn't stay there long. The portal was still open.

I felt the presence of a second immortal demon emerging from the portal. Normally, I'd be horrified, but my Fae form felt . . . emotionless. I flicked my finger, and the second demon fell back into the portal. I only caught a glimpse of glowing blue eyes and long black hair, then it was gone.

Was I that strong, or were they that weak?

Was it a trap of some sort?

The demons were fast. Both of them began coming back to this world, expanding out of the portal like smoke. I reached out with intangible hands and grabbed their expanding essence, claiming it. The flame of darkness that was feeding my rage knew what I wanted.

Torture them, it purred. Make them pay for what they did.

My psychic hands crackled with electricity, and the demons screamed in pain.

An emotion re-entered my head—worry. Was I hurting them? I never meant to! I forced the flame of darkness away, snuffing it out. My all-encompassing rage lessened. I no longer wanted to punish Gonzäro or the other demon. All I needed to do was send them to Inferna, not torture them! Max's death was one thing . . . and I would never forgive Gonzäro for that, but there was no going back from vengeance, from actually torturing someone, no matter how evil they were.

Now that I was slightly more in control of myself, I knew my highest priority was to send the demons back to Inferna and hopefully close the portal as well. I pulled the essence of Gonzäro and the other demon back and stuffed it into the portal, holding it there with one psychic hand.

I said the first words that came to my mind, a spell to close the portal. The spell itself was a formality—I could simply think something to make it happen—but this was a new body with new powers, and the sane part of me decided not to experiment with a task as important as this one. (The rage that could destroy universes was probably also something I needed to be careful with.) It was a pre-made spell from a source I did not know: *"Kameta ashbir hor Aelkiram, estieh portuam seiteyeh exia alakazam estia."*

With a flash, the rift in the volcano portal sealed itself again. Another seal appeared above it, and another—a pillar of magical seals rising into the sky, each one bigger than the one below it.

I looked around. My friends gaped at me in awe. Suddenly, I felt normal. My emotions, my sense of self rushed back. I found myself in my normal body again, feeling cold and exhausted, and collapsed to the ground.

Wait, my clothes had burned off when I transformed. Did that mean I was . . . I didn't have . . . clothes?

I didn't know why I was worrying about that right after I had defeated an immortal demon and resurrected my best friend. Maybe it was like . . . my emotions and personality trying to readjust themselves to my mind, worrying about silly things that the old me would worry about—the me who didn't have the weight of the world thrust on his shoulders when he discovered this magical land.

I lay there, unable to move a muscle. My friends ran to me. The world spun. I could feel myself losing consciousness. My friends stood over me as darkness overtook me. Their clothes were tattered and covered in soot. Korukan was covered in leaves from the portal's "belch," and Lia's clothes were pure black where they had once been green, but they all looked happy. The last thing I saw was a tearfully smiling Nessa, looking fashionable even in her sooty clothes. Of course her clothes were less sooty, tattered, and burned than everyone else's.

CHAPTER 17

Phantasia

"Benvole fentessa, Khioneus."

I felt sleepy. I couldn't hear properly. I slowly came to, as if pulling myself out of thick tar. I was in a circular courtyard that had a floral mosaic on the floor. The courtyard was framed by Grecian-style marble pillars with archways at intervals—the kind you'd see in, I guess, the Taj Mahal or something. There was no roof. I saw trees beyond the pillars and arches, vibrant and other-worldly, with leaves like maple and bark like redwood.

In front of me sat a throne. It had many paintings over its armrests depicting people and animals doing everyday, medieval things, like cooking in pots or getting water from a well.

And the woman on the throne . . . Long ago, when I saw Triskén's face in the Moon, and a woman with butterfly wings appeared—this was her. She was beautiful, her face framed with long silver curls. She didn't look older than thirty. Her crystalline wings were cyan, the color of Aethelum. Her dress shimmered in many colors like an abalone shell. She had a silver circlet on her head with fifteen differently colored gems, the largest one a blue-green gem in the center of the crown.

She smiled. *"Arivali, Khioneus, anyscus ðanfetura."*

"Um . . . I don't mean to be rude, but . . . I don't understand what you're saying."

"Dey mattuna, Khioneus? Frex dopetram can understand me if you concentrate. You are a Semideus after all."

"So I am a Semideus?" I said, marveling that I could understand her now. "Uh, who are you? And why am I wearing a tunic?" I then realized I also had a glowing tail and angel wings, like in my Fae form.

"I am Tïtania, queen of the Fae. Your appearance is your Fae soul, and you are wearing traditional Fae garb, for you are in Phantasia."

Whoa. Phantasia, the kingdom of Fae. Tïtania, the queen.

I looked around and walked beyond the archways toward the small forest, where I laid my hand on a tree. I could feel a thrum, consistent, like a pulse. The pulse of the universe? No, not the universe. It was the pulse of all the universes. I could feel each individual one within the heart of the tree.

Tïtania stood next to me. "I am contacting you while
you are unconscious. Your friends are taking you home.
You used a lot of power in your Magemotican form.

"You are a special creature with a complex destiny
ahead of you. No one, not even the Fae, knows why
Semidei are chosen. A force from the time when this universe was naught but energy chooses them for an
unknowable destiny. They are usually human but with
the divine heart of a Fae. Only one Semideus can exist at
a time. When a Semideus dies, their Fae soul leaves their
body and looks for another worthy host. One of the great
Semidei of the past was Myrddin Wyllt, known to you as
Merlin Ambrosius, the greatest wizard of all time."

It was a lot to take in, but Tïtania was not finished.
"Along with the Semideus there is also a Semidaemon.
This is why I needed to contact you—to warn you. The
Semidaemon has already surfaced in this world, but I
cannot tell you who it is, for such knowledge may change
your future for the worse.

"The Semidaemon is the opposite of the Semideus.
Merlin's foe was Vivian Nimue Fuigna, the most powerful dark wizard of all time. She conquered all of
Pyrhithya and killed so many people and would have
killed so many more if Merlin hadn't stopped her. The
Semidaemon can create all manner of curses, understand the language of the demons, and kill in the same
way the Semideus can bring life. They are unholy, with
the heart of a demon. It is part of the Semideus'

destiny to defeat the Semidaemon and protect the world from it.

"But the Semidaemon is not so different from the Semideus, just as Fae and demons are not so different. And when a Semideus' thoughts become dark, their magic can pluneutralize and become dark magic—in essence, they become a Semidaemon. This is temporary, but it can become permanent if the Semideus loses his sense of who he is—his humanity. Each time the Semideus pluneutralizes from extreme rage, such as when you avenged Maximillis—yes, you almost became a demon when you did that—he loses a bit of his humanity in exchange for power. You are lucky you controlled your desire for vengeance so completely. I was afraid you would turn . . . but that rage gave you the power to send the demons back to Inferna, so perhaps I should be thankful for it."

I already had to deal with my life as a prince of Neurazia and my life on Earth—now being a Semideus, fated to defeat or be defeated by the incarnation of a demon?

I felt so . . . underdressed. Metaphorically speaking. I felt like I was about to walk on the moon with nothing but a T-shirt and shorts.

And what I had done for Max. . . . Were my friends basically immortal? Would I resurrect everyone who died? Was it my choice to make?

I worried. Was there a life-for-a-life situation, where, like, the fact that I brought Max back meant I'd have to kill someone in the future? Did I give myself bad karma? Lose my humanity? I asked Tïtania, "Is there a price for bringing someone back to life?"

"It depends on you," she said cryptically. "The rules are different for every Semideus."

I knew I had to promise myself that I would destroy the Semidaemon, to keep it from hurting others. I had to kill it, even if it killed me.

I hated the thought.

But if the Semidaemon was so evil . . . I would have to do a scary thing like that. I would have to kill it. Even if killing another human meant I lost my own humanity.

But . . . who was the Semidaemon? Understand the language of the demons . . . heart of a demon . . . unholy. The Semidaemon would be shunned by everyone if they knew who it was . . . just like . . .

No. It was not her.

Nessa was a good person. An amazing person. She couldn't be the Semidaemon. She was something different. She had to be. Maybe she was like Furorde with a demonic amulet. Or maybe she was, like, half demon, somehow (though that would mean I was half demon too, unless some bizarre gene-editing weirdness was going on). But she was not a Semidaemon. I was not going to kill my beloved sister.

Yet I couldn't shake the idea that it might be true. That she might be evil. That she might have been lying to me and plotting to kill me.

What if she didn't know what she was? Maybe she was struggling with her Semidaemoniacal powers, wondering whether something was wrong with her.

Maybe it was her "unknowing crime."

Tïtania gave me a serious look. "You must return now. You used much magic in your Magemotican Form, and Gonzäro's attack was filled with dark magic. You will experience intense pain as you descend back into your own body. But it will pass, bringing a long period of unconsciousness, where you will dream of possible futures, like prophecies. Unlike prophecies, these will be futures that may not come to pass. Dispulli, Khioneus."

She touched my forehead. I smelled the scent of freshly baked cake.

Suddenly, every cell in my body exploded. Lava burned my insides. I couldn't breathe. It was hard to think through the pain. White noise rumbled so loudly the building in my head crumbled.

Through the haze of pain, I could make out a ruined building beneath a fiery sky, surrounded by winged creatures. In horror, I realized it was the Temple of Psymus, and it was falling apart. The winged creatures were demons. Dust choked the air, and gargantuan figures rose through the clouds. One slashed at the building. Another fought off pinpricks of light zipping around it. A third, enormous demon with huge horns, a snake tail, and red, pupil-less eyes swung her enormous sword at a glowing figure on the ground. The small figure pushed the giant sword back with its own, despite the size difference.

Then, a demon appeared next to me—silhouetted in the dust and smoke. Pointy shapes stuck out on the demon's head, like horns or ears. A long tail swished behind it. Bright, glowing eyes cut through the haze, and its fangs glinted. Suddenly, it leapt toward me. Just before the dust cleared to reveal the demon's face, the vision ended in darkness.

But, horribly, a part of me knew I would recognize the face if I'd seen it.

Other visions crowded into my head, flashing by like scenery in the window of a train. I caught a glimpse of Nessa's face and some kind of draconian-horse monster. I saw the face of a girl with honey-blonde hair and soft features, her lips full and red. But her beauty was perverted by the evil in her dark blue eyes. They had a coldness in them, like ocean abysses with monsters lurking inside. She smiled at me sinisterly. I could only read her lips, but I think she said, "I know it hurts. But I intend it to."

The horrid pain returned. I sat up, gasping, in a bed. I looked around. Everyone from the Wildlandes trip sat around me, looking relieved. I saw Max, alive and well, and I was so happy.

I looked down and realized I was wearing a tunic, the traditional Fae garb. As if sensing my question (or possibly actually sensing my question), Max said, "You were wearing it after that . . . thing you did. Your skin was hot, and the tunic was smoking so we didn't try to treat you except by pouring healing potions in your mouth from a safe distance away. We had to enchant the bed to make it fireproof. You've been unconscious for ten days." He sighed. "But you're alive, and for that I am very glad."

"Ten days?" I said in shock.

Max nodded. "What happened, anyway? Nessa sensed a dream connection, as if someone was using a dream to contact you, but that was nine days ago. Then you writhed like you were in pain, but the rest of the time, you've been comatose."

"Wow," I said. I looked at Max. "What . . . what do you remember?"

"Me?" Max looked surprised. "What do you mean?"

"After, you know, I was sacrificed, and all that," I said.

"Oh," he said, breaking eye contact with me. "I remember that the demon shot light at me, and this half-naked guy appeared with wings. He was guiding me to these carved, iron gates in the middle of a barren gray desert when this giant, glowing hand appeared out of nowhere pulled me away from him. I feel like I'd sound silly saying this . . . but in Elklorian myth, angels are supposed to fly you to the gates of Prekt's realm for the Judgement. Did I . . . die?"

I looked down at my hands, suddenly feeling self-conscious. "Well . . . yes. I'm a Semideus. I uh . . . brought you back to life."

Furorde, the blue-haired boy with the demonic necklace, frowned. "You're . . . what?"

"A Semideus."

"Um . . . but they don't exist. They're mythological figures."

"So are the gods in your stories, but you guys seem to accept they exist," I said.

Nessa gave me a look like I had said something absurd. "The gods are real beings!"

I shrugged. "My point exactly. If you believe they exist, you should be able to believe Semidei exist. Merlin himself was one."

I then recounted everything Tïtania had said. I noticed Nessa looked disturbed. I couldn't help looking at her while I mentioned the Semidaemon.

I repeated to them what Tïtania told me about how my dreams were visions of futures that may or may not happen. Then I described the visions of the Temple of Psymus falling down and the girl with cruel eyes.

Nessa looked horrified. "Stopping a demon attack on Neurazia in the future will not be an easy feat!"

Korukan spoke. "I think I will place a no-speaking enchantment on all of us. I will tell the king and queen of Neurazia about Khi being a Semideus, and perhaps even the high king and queen of Elkloria, but this is a secret between us, and everyone who knows it will have the no-speaking enchantment. Khi's already known to be a prophet, and that's all anyone should know about him."

Everyone nodded.

No one was mentioning the mysterious, sinister girl I saw in that vision. Why had that vision jumped out at me in particular, while the others just blurred by?

CHAPTER 18

Earth

AFTER I RECOVERED, METARA, MAX, AND I returned to Earth through the Norikithintes Portal. We went accompanied by Korukan and a few wizards whom I did not know, for protection.

Since Max was now safe, Mother and Father decided that for the time being, I needed to return to Earth. Not only did I, according to them, need to continue my Earth education, but I had also been safer on Earth than in Elkloria—as was shown by the fact that I'd been attacked multiple times since coming here. I kind of wanted to stay in Elkloria . . . but at the same time, I was starting to feel homesick for the home I had grown up in, that I had known my whole life.

I had also made a promise to Nessa, to one day take her to Earth and show her what life was like here.

And so, Nessa came with us. She disliked the name Earth—"Who would name a planet after the *ground*?" She also said that calling people from Earth *earthlings* was stupid because an earthling was an elemental creature from Everestera, the kingdom of earth. Nessa brought a stack of magic textbooks and a small black cat named Imi-Nixa who she said was a stray she had taken in.

On Earth, Nessa had black hair that was almost blue, and it was shorter than in Elkloria.

As we stepped through the portal, I could feel my magic fading. It scared me, and I asked Nessa what happened. She said that when we crossed to Vhestibulium, the seraphim, a class of angels from the angel kingdom Revianima, placed "detectors" on our magic so we would not use it irresponsibly. We could still use magic to deal with serious issues, like malevolent magical entities, but if we used it casually, there would be some kind of punishment, like removal of magic. The only magic we could use whenever we wanted was telepathy.

I wondered how many wizards there were in Truckee. Was it just Metara, Max, and me, or were there more? Everyone could be a wizard, for all I knew. Like, Mrs. Jimenez's cooking could have been magical—it was *delicious* . . . but that would have been an irresponsible use of magic, so probably not. Then again, Truckee had a portal to the homeland of wizards, so it would make sense if there were more . . .

✦ ✦ ✦

Nessa adjusted quickly to life in Truckee. She met Sarina and told me the girl was actually a wizard of Avilonéa, the kingdom of air magic, who had the rare power to use magic on Earth for anything at all without punishment.

Nessa had made some friends at school and gone to some dances. People liked her accent (I had also gotten a slight accent from spending my winter in Elkloria, though it faded after a while), and she was way too advanced for her classes—and, of course, she got the attention of many of the boys. Chris Summers, a sophomore and one of the most popular kids in school frequently told me my sister was super hot, and it annoyed me to no end, but I didn't want to tell him that and be impolite. Chris was probably the biggest flirt in the school and officially the "hottest guy." Technically, he elected himself as the hottest guy, but the opinion was shared by several girls.

Mom and Dad freaked out about my adventures in Elkloria and the fact that I joined the NOTT and got myself into several situations where I could have died. Eventually, they calmed down (after yelling at me about the dangers of demons) and told me not to get hurt, but they said they were very proud of me—I had faced off with Triskén, a warlock, a mortal demon, and a wyvern, after all. I even saved Max, with Nessa's help. Of course, I couldn't tell them the Semideus thing because of the no-speaking spell. My throat closed up every time I tried.

Over the next few weeks, Nessa, Metara, Max, and I went through the textbooks Nessa had brought to teach me more magic after school. I had had painfully little education of the sort during Max's kidnapping. I didn't get to cast any of the spells, but I learned the methods.

One day, someone new moved into our neighborhood. Someone I knew.

"KHI! Oh my GOD, it's YOU! This is totally crazy!" exclaimed Angeline after she opened the door. I had come out to greet the new neighbor, but she wasn't as new as I'd thought. "This is a super cool coincidence, huh? We moved here for my dad's work, and this just happens to be where you live!"

We soon were trading stories, some of mine about Elkloria, since she knew all about that, and some of hers about the Wildlandes before she met me. I was glad to have Angeline back. She was in my class, too. We talked after school a lot.

⚜ ⚜ ⚜

NESSA KEPT DISAPPEARING AT NIGHT AND would come back in the morning through the window. The first few nights, I was awoken by a series of clunks in Nessa's room (it had formerly been the guest room, right next to mine). Mom and Dad's room was at the end of the hall, so they didn't hear it.

I decided to stay up, watching for her from my window. I saw her silhouette emerge from her window. Her eyes flashed gold, reflecting moonlight, and I got the uncanny feeling she had seen me and didn't care. It worried me that Nessa was sneaking out, but I was scared to confront her. I came up with ridiculous theories: she was being mind-controlled, someone was masquerading as her, she was the Semi—

No. I stopped myself. She was not evil. I refused to believe that she might not be my annoying yet loving sister. That she might be plotting to kill me.

The next day, after school, Angeline was at my door. "I need to show you something in the forest," she said.

We went to the forest. "This is what I wanted to show you." She pointed to a tree on which there were a few drops of red liquid.

I put my hand over my mouth in shock. "Is that—?"

Angeline nodded. "Looks like blood to me. Can any of your magical senses tell whose it is?"

I shook my head. "I'm no expert at forensics, magical or not, but . . . " I pointed deeper into the forest at another tree with blood on it. "I think we can follow the trail."

Angeline nodded, and we followed. The blood spatters ended in a sort of cave—an overhang opening into a low, dark tunnel. It looked foreboding, but we knew what we had to do. We entered the cave.

CHAPTER 19

Betrayal

ANGELINE AND I CRAWLED INTO THE tunnel and kept crawling, until we came out in an impossible cavern—far too big to fit in the flat forest back in Truckee.

In the center of the cavern was a huge crystalline formation, blood-red and glowing, surrounded by a circle of big gray panels. Inside the crystal was a dark shape. We walked between two of the panels into the circle, and I realized they were not panels at all but mirrors. In the center of the circle, looking up at the crystals stood a girl with long black hair that had an almost blue sheen.

I ran over to her. "Nessa!" I cried. "What are you doing here?"

She turned to me. There was a strange, cold light in her eyes. "Hello, Khi. You should not be here."

"What do you mean?" I asked.

"I mean that you should not have seen any of this. Now I'll be forced to kill you."

"What?" I spluttered.

Nessa held up her hand. "You've seen too much. You must die. Both of you. **Cäthhäx.**"

Dark purple energy shot out of her hand. I tackled Angeline to get her out of the way. The spell shot past me, right between two mirrors, leaving a crater and rubble.

That was dark magic. Wizards couldn't use dark magic.

The Semidaemon can create all manner of curses.

All those times I thought Nessa was keeping secrets —the runes she could read, the suspicions I had forced down . . .

"You really are the Semidaemon," I whispered as I stood up.

"Yes." She smirked. "It is my mission to kill the Magemotican. And I will carry out that mission."

She shot another spell at me. I raised a magical shield, since I was in sufficient danger to do so without prosecution from the seraphim. I didn't know what to feel—betrayal, anger, sadness . . . My sister was the Semidaemon. I had to kill her. But I knew I couldn't, even if she was trying to kill me.

"Nessa," I said. "Stop. Why are you doing this?" There was wetness at the corners of my eyes.

She shot another spell, which I blocked with the shield. I got the feeling she was toying with me. Nessa was way more powerful than me. There was no way that I could hold off against her if she were giving it her all. Did my Semideus powers augment my ability to fight her or something? Or was her humanity holding her back? Maybe she was being mind-controlled, and the real Nessa was trapped in there.

Nessa smiled sinisterly, and I couldn't help but be reminded of that girl in the vision.

"I'm doing it because I want to kill you. I never liked you, Khi. You were so annoying. I hated pretending to love you while I plotted to kill you. And when I discovered what I was in the Wildlandes . . . well, I knew I had all the tools I needed to do just that."

Her words stung, but they made no sense. She couldn't have acted good since day one. Didn't Neurazia have all sorts of truth detection and mind magic? How could she hide? And I did *not* believe, even for a second, that she just "turned to the dark side" in the Wildlandes. Nessa would have been torn apart by the revelation that she was a Semidaemon.

There was some sort of dark magic on her, forcing her to act this way. But where was it from?

I was about to shoot a Nocolco spell to knock her unconscious, but she shot one at me first. I blocked it. She was still playing with me. I needed to try to bring out the real Nessa somehow.

I knew a spell to force someone to speak the truth, having learned it from Nessa's magic textbooks in our after-school lessons. Maybe it would help me find out why Nessa wasn't herself. Or else it would show . . .

Don't think about that.

"**Vocalum Vetatia**," I said. The spell shot at Nessa. Nessa moved out of the way, and the spell hit a mirror and reflected off. The spell zipped around the circle of mirrors, reflecting off of each, until it slammed right back into Nessa, who fell back.

But now I saw something strange. The reflections in the mirrors had become darker than they should have been, permeated with star-like sparkles. I couldn't see Nessa in them. Instead, the mirrors showed a shimmering cyan humanoid. I looked closer . . .

Angeline wasn't in the mirrors, either. In her place was . . . the girl I had seen in my vision.

The spell was meant to make Nessa tell me the truth, but it had caused the mirrors to reveal the truth behind the magic around me. In the reflections, the blood-red crystal was translucent, and trapped inside . . . was Nessa.

I whipped around to face Angeline. She smiled cruelly. Her body glowed, and she transformed into the girl from the vision.

"Who are you," I said shakily, "and what have you done with Angeline?"

"Oh, but, Khi," said the girl. "I *am* Angeline."

She transformed back. "I always was. Angeline never existed."

"You're lying." My voice came out a lot more emotional than I meant it to be.

"Nope!" She grinned.

She *couldn't* be telling the truth. I searched for some sort of reasoning. "Excalibur would never have chosen you unless your intentions were selfless! You wouldn't have been able to wield it! You must have done something to the real Angeline!"

"Actually," said not-Angeline, "that wasn't Excalibur."

The sword she'd told us was Excalibur appeared in her hand. "I made this sword out of evil and shadows. Do you remember Nessa saying she could read the glyphs on the sword? Yes, I *do* know that she said that and many things besides. I have watched you for a long time. I tried to leave clues to help you figure out the truth, but you disregarded them."

She laughed. "I charmed your heart, I suppose."

Anger, numbness, horror—all those feelings from when I thought Nessa had betrayed me came back. Tears flashed in my eyes. I cast Ofensia before I even realized what I was doing. The magic projectile stopped right before it hit her, subliming instantly.

Her eyes darkened, and she floated up, repeating the words from my vision. "I know it hurts. But I intend it to. Angeline doesn't exist. It was always me. Nessa—the real Nessa—is in that sanguinastone over there. The stone is slowly absorbing her magic and life energy. When the stone is clear, Nessa will die."

My face paled, and I looked back at the sanguinastone. It was quite opaque, but for how long? Anger at Angeline's betrayal flooded my senses. Its severity took me by surprise, and in a deep part of my mind, I knew my magic was beginning to pluneutralize, turning me into something like a Semidaemon. Part of me didn't care. Angeline . . . wasn't even Angeline.

"You're the Semidaemon, aren't you . . . whatever your name is?"

She shrugged and smiled. "Semidaemon is an odd word. I always hated Latin—such a nasty-sounding language. You can call me the *Conmanväcsisugco*—or rather, the Dark Goddess. Like Morgana the Fey, ancient enemy of Merlin and sister to that useless, nonmagical king, Arthur Pendragon."

"You're not a goddess," I snarled. I suddenly remembered the part of the prophecy about the goddess of dark and wondered how much of the prophecy was about Angeline.

"It's a fitting name. My powers are godly, unlike yours. I am your nemesis, Khi, you poor little weakling, and you're no match for me."

"Why not kill me now?" I asked.

"Patience. The time shall come for your glorious death," she said. Her shark-like smile reminded me of Triskén. "For now, I have other things that I desire for you, and the time will soon come for you to be part of my plans."

The girl who was once Angeline pointed at the sangui-nastone. "I can get her out of there if you like. I have no use for her anymore—nor for you at the moment. I love toying with people's emotions. It's quite fun."

Suddenly, the cavern disappeared. I was standing on the forest floor, the girl I had thought was Angeline standing next to me. Nessa lay on the ground a few feet away. Her clothes were torn, her skin pale, but she opened her eyes.

She got up groggily. "Khi?"

The sleepiness vanished from her eyes when she saw Angeline. "Khi, get away from her! She's not Angeline!"

"I know," I said quietly. "What about you? Are you okay?"

"Khi," Nessa said. "Get away from her. Please. She's dangerous. She can fool my lie detection magic, and she did some sort of . . . I don't know, lie diversion spell."

I looked at Angeline.

"You're smart," she said. "You'll find me. Maybe you'll even learn my name someday. Maybe you already know it. But we *will* meet again. I give you my word as a goddess of dark magic."

"You're not a goddess! I refuse to call you that!" I yelled. "You . . . Semidaemon!"

The idea of Angeline being the Semidaemon, strangely, made me feel relieved. Nessa was still a mystery, but at least she wasn't the most evil force in the universes.

Angeline winked. "What makes someone a goddess, anyway? Elklorians worship the silly mystical beings created by the Fae at the dawn of this universe, but the Elklorian gods aren't worth worship. They don't even intervene in our lives, yet they get credit for every miraculous event that happens. I would intervene. I would bless those who did good and curse those who did wrong."

"You're delusional."

Angeline smirked. "For the record, I did like you. I still do."

She blew me a kiss. Yuck. I remembered the kiss "Angeline" had given me in the Wildlandes. I was so moonstruck, but now I looked back on it with disgust.

"You're so trusting," Angeline said, noticing the look on my face. "It was fun breaking your heart. And as a parting gift . . . "

She walked toward me. I backed away, holding up my hands to protect myself, but the sizzling spell shot out of her finger too fast for me to stop it. It landed on my shirt near the collar, burning away the material and exposing a faint birthmark high on my left pectoral, near the center of my chest. It wasn't a birthmark, though. It was one of my Bimorphizm symbols—the human symbol. Her fingertips sparked with magic, and the symbol changed from a human silhouette to a glowing fleur-de-lis of the Fae.

My whole body began to glow. I panicked, trying to cast Ofensia but unable. Then my body went rigid, and I couldn't move. I felt cold. Something took shape in the glow emitted by my body—a silhouette moving toward Angeline's fingertips . . . my Fae form.

I cried out and tried to reach for it, but I couldn't move my hand. I tried a telekinesis spell, but again, it didn't work.

Angeline laughed. "Oh, don't worry. I'm only stealing one form. You'll live. Your magic will work—even your Semideus powers. But you won't be able to become a Fae. I'm changing the game a little."

With that, she disappeared into mist, as did my Fae form. My omnipotence was gone.

My power of resurrection was gone.

I ran over to Nessa. "Are you alright?" I said anxiously.

I suddenly stopped and then backed away from her. "What were you doing down there?" I asked suspiciously. My mind was at war with itself. My heart was telling me to stop acting so suspicious—this was Nessa. But a particularly nasty part of my mind was saying, *You can't trust your heart. Your heart told you Angeline was an amazing person and look how that turned out.*

Nessa looked mystified. "I . . . don't know. I just . . . I met Angeline while walking home, and we started a conversation, but then I . . . fell unconscious."

"Unconscious?" I asked skeptically.

"Days ago, I woke up in that weird cavern. Angeline was standing over me. She said, 'Comply with my demands or your brother dies. I have cast a curse on him that will kill him whenever I want.' I went home and tried removing the curse from you while you slept, but she appeared in my head and threatened to kill you right away. And then . . . she told me to sneak out of the house every night and collect these different ingredients from the forest.

"She said if you saw me, I had to ignore it. And this morning, she pushed me into the sanguinastone we created from the ingredients. I couldn't stop her. She was too powerful!"

My heart finally won. My voice thickened with emotion. "Thank goodness you're okay," I whispered.

"Forget about me. Are you okay?"

Confused, I said, "Why wouldn't I be?"

"I know the pain of betrayal, but I don't think you have felt it before."

She was right. Something had changed in me, and not just the lack of my Fae form. I felt harder, closed off. I'd been too trusting. I should've known better than to trust a random girl in the Wildlandes. The *Wildlandes*. I'd always been a little gullible—I never could stop myself from feeling sympathy for someone even if they did nothing more than pretend to cry.

"Well, whatever. It doesn't matter. I'm fine," I said. It was definitely a lie.

"But . . . your Fae form . . . "

"In the end, it only mattered when Max died, and the demon freed himself from Inferna. The portal closed, and Max is alive, so why do I need it anymore?

And she's the Semidaemon. Besides, I didn't have a crush on her."

Did I? She did kiss me. Ugh, I didn't understand crushes. I didn't understand any of this.

"Thanks for not saying 'I told you so,'" I said, after a pause.

⚜ ⚜ ⚜

THE NEXT DAY, I FOUND OUT her house had vanished, along with her parents. Totally gone.

"Angeline-Marena Feerique?" said my history teacher when taking attendance. She tapped her clipboard with her pen. "The chart says she sits next to Alex . . . "

"No one sits next to me," said Alex, frowning.

"Huh," replied my teacher. "Who's this? A new student? I'll have to ask the attendance office about her."

Angeline-Marena Feerique doesn't exist, I wanted to say.

I thought of Max. How he'd kept the fact that he was gay a secret from me since he was eleven. Three entire years. I couldn't imagine what that must have been like.

Now that I knew about Elkloria, about being a Semideus, about false Angeline—I had to lie. Lying had never been in my nature. I didn't want to lie to everyone.

But now, with all of Elkloria to think about . . . I could never be truly honest again.

About the Author

RISHAB BORAH has held a deep passion for magic and mystical things since elementary school. He started creating the world "Elkloria" when he was 11. Besides writing, Rishab is also an accomplished artist and loves to sketch wildlife, imaginary mythological figures, and dragons. He has a keen interest in linguistics, science, and programming—he recently taught himself Python and Java programming in order to create his own video games. He currently lives with his parents in the Silicon Valley, California area.

RECENT AND FORTHCOMING BOOKS FROM THREE ROOMS PRESS

FICTION

Rishab Borah
The Door to Inferna

Meagan Brothers
Weird Girl and What's His Name

Christopher Chambers
Scavenger

Ron Dakron
Hello Devilfish!

Robert Duncan
Loudmouth

Michael T. Fournier
Hidden Wheel
Swing State

William Least Heat-Moon
Celestial Mechanics

Aimee Herman
Everything Grows

Eamon Loingsigh
Light of the Diddicoy
Exile on Bridge Street

John Marshall
The Greenfather

Aram Saroyan
Still Night in L.A.

Richard Vetere
The Writers Afterlife
Champagne and Cocaine

Julia Watts
Quiver

Gina Yates
Narcissus Nobody

MEMOIR & BIOGRAPHY

Nassrine Azimi and Michel Wasserman
*Last Boat to Yokohama: The Life and
Legacy of Beate Sirota Gordon*

William S. Burroughs & Allen Ginsberg
*Don't Hide the Madness:
William S. Burroughs in Conversation
with Allen Ginsberg*
edited by Steven Taylor

James Carr
*BAD: The Autobiography of
James Carr*

Richard Katrovas
*Raising Girls in Bohemia:
Meditations of an American Father*

Judith Malina
*Full Moon Stages:
Personal Notes from
50 Years of The Living Theatre*

Phil Marcade
*Punk Avenue: Inside the New York City
Underground, 1972–1982*

Alvin Orloff
*Disasterama! Adventures in the Queer
Underground 1977–1997*

Nicca Ray
*Ray by Ray: A Daughter's Take
on the Legend of Nicholas Ray*

Stephen Spotte
*My Watery Self:
Memoirs of a Marine Scientist*

PHOTOGRAPHY-MEMOIR

Mike Watt
On & Off Bass

SHORT STORY ANTHOLOGIES

SINGLE AUTHOR

The Alien Archives: Stories
by Robert Silverberg

First-Person Singularities: Stories
by Robert Silverberg
with an introduction by John Scalzi

Tales from the Eternal Café: Stories
by Janet Hamill, with an introduction
by Patti Smith

*Time and Time Again:
Sixteen Trips in Time*
by Robert Silverberg

*Voyages:
Twelve Points of Departure*
by Robert Silverberg

MULTI-AUTHOR

*Crime + Music: Twenty Stories
of Music-Themed Noir*
edited by Jim Fusilli

Dark City Lights: New York Stories
edited by Lawrence Block

*The Faking of the President: Twenty
Stories of White House Noir*
edited by Peter Carlaftes

*Florida Happens:
Bouchercon 2018 Anthology*
edited by Greg Herren

*Have a NYC I, II & III:
New York Short Stories;*
edited by Peter Carlaftes
& Kat Georges

*Songs of My Selfie:
An Anthology of Millennial Stories*
edited by Constance Renfrow

*The Obama Inheritance:
15 Stories of Conspiracy Noir*
edited by Gary Phillips

*This Way to the End Times:
Classic and New Stories of
the Apocalypse*
edited by Robert Silverberg

MIXED MEDIA

John S. Paul
Sign Language: A Painter's Notebook
(photography, poetry and prose)

FILM & PLAYS

Israel Horovitz
*My Old Lady: Complete Stage Play
and Screenplay with an Essay on
Adaptation*

Peter Carlaftes
Triumph For Rent (3 Plays)
Teatrophy (3 More Plays)

Kat Georges
*Three Somebodies: Plays about
Notorious Dissidents*

DADA

*Maintenant: A Journal of
Contemporary Dada Writing & Art*
(Annual, since 2008)

TRANSLATIONS

Thomas Bernhard
On Earth and in Hell
*(poems of Thomas Bernhard
with English translations by
Peter Waugh)*

Patrizia Gattaceca
Isula d'Anima / Soul Island
*(poems by the author
in Corsican with English
translations)*

César Vallejo | Gerard Malanga
Malanga Chasing Vallejo
*(selected poems of César Vallejo
with English translations
and additional notes by
Gerard Malanga)*

George Wallace
EOS: Abductor of Men
(selected poems in Greek & English)

ESSAYS

Home Is the Mouth of a Shark
Vanessa Baden

*Womentality: Thirteen Empowering Stories
by Everyday Women Who Said Goodbye to
the Workplace and Hello to Their Lives*
edited by Erin Wildermuth

HUMOR

Peter Carlaftes
A Year on Facebook

POETRY COLLECTIONS

Hala Alyan
Atrium

Peter Carlaftes
DrunkYard Dog
I Fold with the Hand I Was Dealt

Thomas Fucaloro
It Starts from the Belly and Blooms

Kat Georges
Our Lady of the Hunger

Robert Gibbons
Close to the Tree

Israel Horovitz
Heaven and Other Poems

David Lawton
Sharp Blue Stream

Jane LeCroy
Signature Play

Philip Meersman
This Is Belgian Chocolate

Jane Ormerod
Recreational Vehicles on Fire
Welcome to the Museum of Cattle

Lisa Panepinto
On This Borrowed Bike

George Wallace
Poppin' Johnny

Three Rooms Press | New York, NY | Current Catalog: www.threeroomspress.com
Three Rooms Press books are distributed by PGW/Ingram: www.pgw.com